THE VINTAGE BOOKSHOP OF MEMORIES

Elizabeth Holland

ABOUT ELIZABETH HOLLAND

Elizabeth Holland is a keen writer of romance novels. She enjoys the escapism of picking up a book and transporting yourself into a new world. With her mind bursting with lots of different stories Elizabeth is exploring the world of self-publishing her novels.

You can contact Elizabeth on Twitter @EHollandAuthor

Cover design by: Dawn Cox Photography

CHAPTER ONE

Prue smoothed the creases out of her charcoal pencil skirt as she stood up from the church pew. She looked around the small room to see the handful of people that had gathered, all wiping tears from their eyes. It was a bright but cold Wednesday in April and the cemetery was the last place Prue wanted to be. As she glanced around at the mourners Prue wondered how many of them had really known her grandmother. The entire village knew the name Elizabeth Clemonte and yet so few had known the real woman behind the name.

'Prudence, how lovely to see you.' Prue was pulled from her thoughts by the voice of an elderly man. She looked up to see the vicar smiling down at her, he had known Prue her entire life and had even been the one to baptise her. Everyone knew everyone in the little village that she had once called home, they especially knew you if you lived in the big house on the hill. Otherwise known as 'Clemonte Manor'. The village, Ivy Hatch, was nestled amongst the rolling hills of Somerset and was mostly unknown. Each summer a handful of tourists would stumble upon the sleepy village but other than that the only visitors were from local towns or villages.

Prue politely returned the vicar's smile and engaged in some small talk, all the while she just wanted to get out of the stuffy church. Although Prue had been too young to remember her own mother's funeral she had grown up to be somewhat afraid of God's house. The little church was a reminder that she had grown up without a mother by her side. It was only the church that made her feel that way though, the graveyard surrounding it only evoked feeling of peace and contentment. Prue had many fond memories of visiting the graveyard with her grandmother over the years. Each week they would visit the Clemonte mausoleum, that hour spent in the graveyard was the closest Prue ever felt to her grandmother.

Once outside in the cemetery Prue felt her shoulders relax. The few attendees of the funeral service were milling around outside, unsure what to do next. Following her grandmother's wishes Prue had not arranged a wake, both her and her grandmother knew that the majority of the village would come along just to satisfy their curiosity and to see the inside of the Clemonte manor. Prue cast her gaze up to the hill above the village to where her home lay. At least it was once her home, before she went to university, and now it would become her home again.

Only a week ago, Prue had received a call from her grandmother's doctor telling her to come quickly. She had packed up all of belongings and left her house share in Brighton to return to the little village she had once called her home. Prue always knew this day would come, she had just hoped it would be a long way in the future. Despite her grandmother's lack of maternal instinct, she had been the only family member Prue had left. So now at the age of twenty-four Prue was Lady of the Manor with an entire village watching her to see what her next move would be. She knew the residents of Ivy Hatch saw her as an entitled snob, however in reality she was far from it. That's why Prue had loved living in Brighton, nobody had batted an eyelid at how different she was. Her love for 1940s fashion always made her stand out from the crowd. Today, her glossy black hair was in pin curls, one side swept back to show off her petite features. She had dressed for her grandmother's funeral in her favourite pencil skirt and matching jacket with a crisp white shirt underneath. Perhaps she had gone a step too far with her lace gloves, black parasol and a black fascinator, complete with a birdcage veil. It was a little over the top but she knew her grandmother would have appreciated her dressing properly for the occasion. Despite their differences Prue's fashion sense was something that she had inherited from her grandmother who had insisted on dressing up for every occasion.

Prue was acutely aware of the villagers watching her from afar, all whispering about how indifferent she thought she was. If only they could have seen what her life had been like in Brighton, living in a house share with eight other people and spending her days working at the local auction house as a valuer. She had worked hard to forge a career for herself but here she was, back at the manor. Her grandmother's dying wish had been for her to move home, on her deathbed she had reminded Prue the importance of keeping their family name alive. There was also the responsibility of owning the majority of the village.

Relief washed over Prue as she spotted the black hearse pull up, ready to take her home. As her heels clicked on the path below her she held her head up high, thanked the vicar and made her way over to the car. She knew that every pair of eyes were on her, ready for her to mess up in some way. You see the villagers had never liked the Clemontes, they were a reminder of a class system that everyone but Prue's grandmother wanted to forget. However, there were still the odd few who worshipped the system and believed that the Clemontes should be treated differently, Prue didn't much like those people. Even as a child Prue had wondered why everyone couldn't be treated as equals. It was a delicate line to tread and Prue would need to strike a balance between respecting the old fashioned ways whilst also bringing the village into the present.

For now though, all Prue wanted to do was go home and cry, and so she stepped into the hearse ready to go back to the manor. It may have been too big for just her but at least it somewhat felt like home, after all it was all she had ever known. Prue looked out of the window as they passed the back of the cemetery, even from the road she could see the Clemonte family mausoleum.

She lifted her hand and gave a small wave towards her mother's resting place. Oh, she would give almost anything to still have her mother by her side, telling her what to do next.

The hearse drew up to the manor and Prue thanked the driver before getting out and walking up the few steps to the front door. With an ominous creak, Prue pushed open the heavy door and walked into the sparse hallway. Despite her grandmother's lack of maternal instinct she had still been family. She may not have hugged Prue but she always made sure there were staff available to give Prue everything she needed. A single tear fell from Prue's eye as she glanced up at a family portrait, the only one of her grandmother, her mother and her. Prue was only a baby in this picture but she wanted to believe that she still remembered that day. A day when she was surrounded by family.

As another tear fell from her eye, Prue locked the door behind her and headed up to her bedroom, she had a long day ahead of her tomorrow. Prue had been summoned by her grandmother's solicitor. Over the phone he had told Prue that she was the sole heir to the Clemonte estate, however he wanted to see her face-to-face to discuss some of the finer details. With this in mind Prue changed out of her funeral attire and into her emerald green silk pyjamas and climbed into her bed. The room was styled to suit Prue's eclectic taste, it was as if you had stepped back in time into the art deco period. It was Prue's solace in a house that seemed so cold and distant. As Prue's head hit the pillow more tears fell from her eyes, her life had been completely turned upside down and here she was, back in a village where everyone despised her for no fault of her own. Life wasn't going to be easy over the next few months.

CHAPTER TWO

The following morning Prue woke before sunrise. She pulled on her fur coat, made a cup of coffee and went to stand outside on the back terrace. From the manor's spot on the hill she could see down into the village. A few of the little cottages had lights on and smoke billowing from their chimneys. They looked homely and inviting, unlike the cold pile of bricks behind her. Despite her grandmother's attempts to modernise the interior it was still an old property and therefore was often cold and damp. Its sheer size was starting to dawn on Prue now she was the only one living there. She craved the comfort of carpeted floors and deep comfy sofas to sink in to and watch television. The manor's saving grace was its library, a room filled from floor to ceiling with books. Even from a young age Prue had been in her element in that room. There were endless worlds for her to fall into and all she had to do was pick a book and lose herself in the moment. To say Prue was a keen reader would be an understatement, whenever she had a spare moment she could always be found with her head in a book.

Prue stood outside wrapped in her oversized coat, sipping her coffee as she watched the sunrise in the distance. Despite it being April the mornings were still so cold Prue could see her breath linger in the air. She looked out towards the fields, where she could see farmers tending to their animals. It was nice to be back at home in the countryside. Today was her final day in limbo, once she had spoken to her grandmother's solicitor she could then go about rebuilding her life here. Selling the manor was not an option, it had been in the family for too many years, her grandmother had ensured she knew this from a very young age. Prue respected this, after all the manor was her only link to her mother. The manor held endless valuable memories that could never be replaced, for that reason alone it would always be home. However, Prue was determined to make the manor feel a little cosier and homely. She would also find a job at one of the local auction houses. She could probably live off of the income that the estate generated but Prue knew she had to keep working to stay sane. She did not want to risk turning into her grandmother. With a sigh Prue turned and went back inside the house, she had a meeting to get ready for.

What did one wear to a will reading? Were you suppose to dress as though you were going to a funeral? Prue resisted the urge to pick up her phone and text her ex-housemate, after all it was only 8am, she would still be asleep. Instead she settled on a pair of brown tweed waist high flared trousers with a silk cream blouse. She was well aware that her fashion sense was somewhat eccentric but who could blame her growing up in an 18th century manor house, with a grandmother who believed she still ruled the village? Prue was never destined to be normal.

After running a brush through her hair Prue was happy to see that her curls had survived the night. She applied a small amount of make-up and grabbed her handbag ready for her 9am meeting. Walking towards the garage, Prue let out a little squeal of delight. Coming home to the manor meant that she could drive her own car again. Despite not being the most loving of grandmothers, Elizabeth Clemonte had understood her granddaughter very well and so for her eighteenth birthday she had bought her a vintage car. Not just any vintage car though - a vintage Bentley. Prue had been terrified to drive it but now she was back home it was her only mode of transport, so for the time being she was going to drive her vintage car and love every second of it.

Prue found the drive to the solicitor's office to be somewhat calming, once this was over she could focus on organising her life. It was only a short drive of ten miles and the day was beautiful. The sun was high in the sky with not a cloud in sight and despite the cold breeze Prue opened the window slightly and revelled in the fresh air that filled the car. It was a beautiful day and her soul was happy to be home. There was a part of Prue that felt incredibly guilty for feeling so happy about life since it was only yesterday that she buried her grandmother. She couldn't help it though, somewhere deep inside of her she felt as though she was about to embark on the next chapter of her life. She had a whole new adventure stretching out in front of her and she couldn't wait to throw herself into it. That was the kind of girl she was, anything that came her way she embraced it. It would frustrate her grandmother sometimes and Prue was sure this was a trait that she must have inherited from her father. She would never know, with her grandmother dead there was nobody left on earth that could point Prue in the direction of her father. Her mother's indiscretion would forever be a secret with only Prue to show for it.

As Prue pulled up outside the solicitor's office she felt as though she were teetering on the edge of something, but what that something was, she did not know. All she knew was that the solicitor wanted to see her to discuss the estate. With her head held high and her shoulders back, she pushed open the door to the office, oozing a confidence that she definitely wasn't feeling. The receptionist smiled at her and told her to take a seat, Mr Adley would be out to see her soon. Prue wasn't surprised that she hadn't needed to introduce herself, the Clemontes were very well known in the area. Within a few seconds of taking her seat Mr Adley appeared and ushered her into his office.

'Thank you for coming in to see me, Miss Clemonte.' Mr Adley pulled out a seat for her and gestured for her to sit in it. Having lived in Brighton for the past few years Prue had forgotten what it was like to come home and be treated as if she were royalty.

'Please Mr Adley, call me Prue.' She smiled kindly up at the man as she took her seat. He looked to be in his late fifties with a smattering of grey hair on his head. Despite his tired expression his eyes appeared warm and friendly.

'If you don't mind Miss Clemonte, I think it is best if we keep things professional.'

Prue was suitably chastised. She knew her grandmother would have been glaring at her if she had been in the room with her, they were always the Clemontes to the village.

The silence in the room was somewhat awkward as Mr Adley sorted through his paperwork and Prue busied herself looking around the small office. It was dark, with piles of paperwork covering every surface. How Mr Adley could find anything amongst this mess Prue didn't know, she wanted to start sorting through it all whilst he gathered the right paperwork.

'Ahh, here we are. Mrs Elizabeth Clemonte's will.'

Prue had to try really hard to concentrate as Mr Adley read out the name of every building and piece of land that the Clemontes owned. A heavy feeling settled at the bottom of Prue's stomach as she realised that she was now heir to all of this; it was her responsibility to ensure that the farms were run properly, people's jobs were safe and their homes were well kept.

'Miss Clemonte, as you may be aware I oversee all of the legalities of the Clemonte estate and I correspond with your estate manager. Providing you agree, I am happy for this to continue, the only thing you would be required to do is attend the annual meeting.' Prue breathed a sigh of relief, she was more than happy to allow things to continue this way.

'As you know the manor has been left to you, your grandmother has not left any restrictions on that, other than the fact that you're unable to sell it.' That was fine, Prue had been expecting that. Despite everything, she would never wish to sell her home.

'There is one more matter, Miss Clemonte. I'm not sure whether you're aware of the business venture your grandmother owns in town? I believe she inherited it from your mother upon her death.'

Prue leant forward slightly in her chair, she was not aware of any business that her grandmother had inherited from her mother. Come to think of it she was not aware that her mother had ever owned a business in town. Why would her grandmother have kept this from her?

'Your mother, Dorothy Clemonte, owned a bookshop in the heart of the town. I believe there was some controversy around it at the time, the villagers were unhappy at the idea of your mother playing shop. She loved that little place though. After her death your grandmother boarded it up and as far as I'm aware nobody has stepped foot inside since.'

Prue was finding it hard to catch her breath. Her mother had owned a little bookshop in the village and yet she had never known anything about it. The idea that there was a place that had such a connection with her mother filled Prue with excitement. Her mother had been taken from them too soon. She had been born with a heart defect and over the years she had become weaker and weaker, until one day she went into hospital and never came home. At least that was how Prue remembered it, being so young had shielded her from the true trauma of those life-changing days.

Mr Adley gave Prue directions to the shop and handed her a key. It wasn't a new key, it was an old fashioned skeleton key. It was just the key that Prue would have chosen for her own shop. She thanked Mr Adley, as quickly as possible and left the office, feeling as though she was in a dream. There was only one place she wanted to be right now and that was the mysterious bookshop.

CHAPTER THREE

As Prue stepped outside of the office a sickening feeling came over her. What should she do next? She had expected to walk out of the office with her life on track and ready to start job hunting. Instead, here she was feeling confused and excited. She could go straight to the bookshop, however she felt as though she had to prepare herself for that. After a lifetime of believing she would never learn anything more about her mother she had just been presented with a treasure trove of memories. This bookshop would be her mother's vision, an insight into her thoughts and imagination. Prue had to reign her thoughts in, she had to stop herself from getting carried away. For all she knew her grandmother may have had the place gutted and it could just be a shell. She doubted it though. Despite her grandmother's harshness she had adored her only daughter and had done everything she could to keep her memory alive. Prue was aware of something happening that split the mother-daughter bond that the pair had shared, she had always suspected it had something to do with her but she had never sought any answers.

Instead of going straight to the shop Prue decided to park up in the village and pop into the cafe for a drink, before delving into her mother's past. There was only one cafe in town, The Honey Pot, and so Prue headed straight there. She remembered the cafe from her childhood, however back then it was known as The Tea Rooms and the lovely lady that ran it always gave Prue an extra large slice of cake. It was now table service and so Prue pushed the door open and seated herself at one of the tables by the window so she could watch as the villagers passed by.

'Miss Clemonte, what can I get you?' A flustered waitress came running over, coming to an abrupt halt next to the table and doing something between a curtsey and a bow. Prue had to stop herself from laughing at the young girl.

'Please, call me Prue. Could I have a cappuccino and a tea cake please?' Prue smiled up at the girl as she frantically wrote the order down on her notepad.

'Of course Miss Cle... Sorry, I mean Prue. I'll bring it over as soon as it's ready.' With a final smile the girl returned to the counter to put the order in. Prue smiled and returned her gaze to the village outside, there was something so relaxing about people watching. She could feel the eyes of everyone in the cafe staring at her, wondering what her next move would be. Prue suddenly found herself feeling homesick for Brighton. Despite having grown up in the village she had spent the last few years living in Brighton and she had loved every moment of it. Prue had particularly enjoyed blending into the crowds of people with nobody knowing who she or her family were.

In just a few minutes Prue's order was brought over by the same waitress. Feeling a little embarrassed, Prue thanked her and tucked into her late breakfast, her order had definitely skipped the queue. As she bit into her teacake Prue realised why she was receiving such a special service, she now owned the premises. Prue's realisation was cut short as the door to the cafe opened and the little bell above it rung out. In walked a man, who looked to be in his late fifties. He looked as though he would have been quite good looking in his prime, although now his dark locks were greying and his piercing blue eyes were sunken and framed by years of lines. His gaze fell upon her and he began to make his way over to her table, a menacing look on his face.

'Has the lady of the manor deemed herself good enough to sit with us commoners?' He spat at her, he was now stood next to her table towering above her.

'Excuse me?' Prue spluttered, she had known that the villagers didn't particularly like her but she hadn't expected this reaction. The older woman, who had been stood behind the counter, came scurrying over.

'Arnold, not here.' She hissed at him, trying to pull at his arm to drag him away from Prue.

'Wait. This is ridiculous. I live here too so I'd rather clear the air than have to avoid you all whenever I need to pop into town for anything.' Prue's voice sounded a lot braver than she was actually feeling. She remembered what her grandmother had always taught her and sat up straight with her head held high and her shoulders back. Fake confidence was just as effective as real confidence.

'Oh how good of you to grace us with your presence in the village.' The menacing tone of the man's voice had not dampened.

'I'm not gracing you with my presence, I'm simply living here too.' Prue was beginning to get annoyed, how dare this man speak to her like this? He didn't even know her.

'Arnold, I think it might be best if you leave.' The woman sounded stern, she walked over towards the door and opened it for him. With a final glare at Prue he turned on his heel and marched out of the cafe, leaving behind him a silence as everyone waited to see what Prue would do next.

'Does anyone want to tell me what that was about?' Prue addressed her question to the whole cafe, she hoped that someone might be able to explain to her what she had already done wrong. After all, she'd been away from the village for years.

'I'm Wendy, I run The Honey Pot cafe and I suppose I'm also one of your tenants.' The woman moved from the door and sat down opposite Prue, putting her hand out for Prue to shake.

'Prue Clemonte, nice to meet you Wendy.' Prue smiled at her

and took a sip of her coffee, feeling her body begin to relax again.

'It's not you Prue that everyone has a problem with. It's the Clemontes.'

'But I am a Clemonte?' Prue responded, she was beginning to feel more and more confused.

'The thing is dear,' one of the elderly men from a neighbouring table pulled his chair over to them and sat down, 'you've been gone for quite a while.'

'I've been living and working in Brighton.' Prue explained, although why she had to justify her life choices to these complete strangers, she did not know.

'That's fine dear, the problem is people are worried about their livelihoods. Your grandmother, god rest her soul, was a harsh woman but a brilliant landlady. We knew that our futures were safe and we wouldn't wake up one day to find the land our businesses are on had been sold to the highest bidder.' The man finished his explanation and Prue had to admit that she could see his point. The villagers didn't know her and she had been gone for years, they were within their rights to feel worried that she might sell their businesses from under their feet. However, shouting at her in a busy cafe was not the right way to introduce yourself to your new landlady.

'Please believe me when I say this. I have no intention of selling any land or properties. This morning I met with Mr Adley and we have agreed that he will continue to oversee the Clemonte estate. All that has changed is that it is now my name on the deeds rather than my grandmother's. I intend to keep everything the same.' As Prue finished her little announcement she could hear a sigh of relief from everyone in the cafe. She suddenly felt herself feeling a little sick, she was now responsible for all the people's livelihoods. Any future decisions she made impacted on an entire village.

'Wendy, could I have my bill please?' Prue wanted to leave, the walls felt as though they were closing in on her and every set of eyes were watching her every move. She wished she had gone straight to the bookshop, then all of this might have been avoided.

'It's on the house, call it a welcome home present.' Wendy smiled at her.

Prue stood up and grabbed her handbag, as she turned around to look at the rest of the cafe, all heads suddenly turned as if they hadn't been watching her.

'I'm sure you all heard that but just incase you didn't, I don't intend for anything to change. Mr Adley will remain in charge of the estate.' Prue could feel her fake confidence crumbling as she addressed the whole room, she got her words out as quickly as possible before turning on her heel and walking towards the door.

'Oh and Wendy, I don't intend to take advantage of you or your business and so I shall deduct the cost of my breakfast from next month's rent.' With a final glance back at everyone's shocked faces Prue walked back out of the cafe and into the fresh air. She had a new life to adjust to, a business to uncover and a whole village to win over. Prue Clemonte would certainly be busy for the next few months. She was beginning to wish she hadn't turned the page to begin this new chapter of her life.

CHAPTER FOUR

Prue took a deep breath and did her best to forget about what had just happened inside the cafe. With trembling hands she took the skeleton key out of her handbag and followed the directions that Mr Adley had given her to her mother's old bookshop. She followed the main path through the village and took a left just before the church. This church was much bigger than the one at the cemetery and it was home to the weekly service. Prue's grandmother had insisted that they attended the service each Sunday and so they would dress in their best clothes and take their seats at the front of the church. Everyone's eyes were always on them rather than the vicar. As a child Prue had enjoyed the attention, however as she grew older she came to hate the weekly ritual until eventually she put her foot down and refused to go. Her grandmother had been upset but she had understood that Prue didn't want to be involved in the charade anymore. That seemed like a lifetime ago now.

The left hand turn had taken her onto a cobbled street with houses either side, all of which boasted window boxes filled with flowers, just waiting for a spell of warm weather to bloom. The third door on the left was boarded up with just the doorknob and key hole on show. This was it, this was her mother's old bookshop. Prue took a step back to admire the old building. Next to the boarded up doorway there was a window, which was also boarded up. The building itself was made from chunky stones that had been whitewashed. It needed a good clean but there was something awfully quaint about the little place. Prue took a deep breath to steady herself and with trembling hands she unlocked the door and pushed it open, ready to immerse herself in history.

A gasp escaped Prue as she stepped inside the shop. The smell of mustiness hit her senses, as she blinked to adjust to the dim lighting. It was beautiful, a hidden treasure trove of books. If Prue could have designed her dream shop, this would be it. She stepped into the shop, leaving the door open slightly, to allow some light in. A switch was to the left of the door but as she flicked it nothing happened. She would have to make do with the little natural light that the door was letting in. Books lined the walls from the floor to the ceiling. On the back wall stood a balcony, overlooking the entire shop with an old-fashioned ladder leading to it. Prue tiptoed around the room, running her fingers along the spines of all the books, they were thick with dust but they'd be fine after a good clean. There had to be thousands of books in here. She had always known her mother was a keen reader but she hadn't known the true extent of her mother's love for books. To the right of the shop was a counter in the same dark wood as the bookshelves, perched on the top was an old fashioned till. It was beautiful. Prue had come across a few of these during her time working in auction houses, but never had she found one in such pristine condition, at least it would be pristine if it wasn't covered in a layer of dust.

The shop would need a good clean and each individual book would need dusting but there was something magical about it. So many stories to be told, all locked away and forgotten about. Prue wandered over towards the back of the shop where an old leather chair was placed, it would be lovely after a good clean and polish. On the shelves next to the chair were leather bound fairytales. Prue ran her fingers across the spines, moving the dust so that she could see the title of each one. As her hands fell upon Cinderella, she pulled it out and blew the dust off of the cover before opening it up to read the first page. As she opened the book a piece of paper fell out and tumbled to the ground.

Prue knelt down and picked it up, feeling a shiver run down her spine as she recognised the handwriting. It was her mother's. She moved closer to the entrance of the shop so that she could read the words properly.

Good choice, Cinderella was always my favourite fairytale. If you like this and are looking for another fairytale why not try, Sleeping Beauty?

P.S What are the names of the mice?

Lots of love,
Dorothy

Prue could feel her heart hammering in her chest as she read and re-read her mother's few words. They were short and not in any way aimed at her but still it was nice to be reminded of her mother's presence. As Prue glanced around at the towering shelves of books she wondered whether her mother had placed a note inside each one. With trembling hands, Prue reached out to the shelf closest to her, it housed non-fiction books. She chose the book on Egyptian history. With a deep breath Prue opened the cover and out flew a little slip of paper with her mother's handwriting. This time her mother had suggested the reader progress to a fiction book based in ancient Egypt. As Prue slotted the book back into its place on the shelf she looked round at the shop in awe, had her mother really read all of these books and placed a slip of paper in each one to recommend another? It was a small but personal touch and Prue knew that if she had purchased a book and found a similar slip inside she would have been itching to return to buy another.

Feeling overwhelmed, Prue stepped back outside onto the cobbled path to catch her breath. The smell of fresh air was welcome after she had inhaled so much dust. Her mind was at war with itself, part of her wanted to take on the shop and run it as her own but the other half of her reminded her that her speciality was in antiques, not books. She could learn though, couldn't she? After all, she hadn't been born with the knowledge to value items, she had spent many years learning from others and teaching herself. Unsure what to do Prue took the key from her pocket and locked the door. She couldn't make a decision whilst being so close to the shop, her heart would win every time. There was something magical about the place, as though her mother's spirit was living on inside. To make a sensible decision she needed to put some distance between herself and the building. In the meantime though it wouldn't hurt to get an electrician in to sort the lights out. Whether she decided to keep it as a shop or not, she would have to sort it out at some point and some lighting would be helpful.

CHAPTER FIVE

The following day, Prue woke to the sound of her alarm. She rose confused and groggy after having had a few too many gin fizzes last night, whilst trying to decide what to do with the shop. Prue had called a local electrician after leaving the shop and he had agreed to pop in today to have a look at the electrics. That was why Prue was up so early. She was to meet the electrician outside the shop at 8am but before that she needed to stock up on cleaning products. Prue's heart wanted to keep the shop and to run it but her head was all too aware of the problems that would cause. She was clearly disliked amongst the locals and so it was unlikely the shop would thrive. After her fourth gin fizz Prue had decided she may as well clean and tidy the shop, after all it could hardly be rented out in its current state. So with that in mind, Prue had set her alarm for 6am and had celebrated making a decision with a few more cocktails.

With a pounding head, Prue glanced at herself in the mirror, she definitely was looking a little worse for wear. After her numerous cocktails she had fallen into bed around midnight, still in her clothes and make-up. Looking in the mirror now Prue had many regrets. After a quick shower and a coffee she abandoned her usual attire and instead opted to put her hair up, complete with a headscarf, and grabbed some navy high waisted trousers and a matching cropped jumper. This was as put together as she was going to get at this time in the morning. With a glance at her car keys Prue decided to walk into the village. She had to get herself a practical car, it was a little gaudy to drive everywhere in a vintage Bentley.

With the key to the shop safely stowed in her trouser pocket Prue began the walk into the village, the walk home would be unpleasant but at least the walk there was all downhill. The birds were singing from the safety of the branches above her, meanwhile Prue could see a few farmers out in the surrounding fields feeding their livestock. As much as she had loved the vivid life in Brighton she had missed the stillness and laidback way of life in the village. Somehow she had to win over the people if she wanted to stay here. She just wished someone would tell her how she could do that.

After a quick trip to the village shop, Prue stocked up on cleaning products and made her way to the bookshop. Despite the early morning there had still been lots of villagers in the shop, buying their daily paper, all of whom had been talking about her behind her back. Prue had held her head high and hid the unshed tears in her eyes, this was her home too. She wanted to make this work so that she could happily live side-by-side with everyone.

Prue's pace picked up as she got closer and closer to the bookshop, she was yearning for the solace of those towering book shelves and the musty smell of old books. The bookshop would be her sanctuary for the time being, a place where she could shut herself away and think about what she was going to do with her life. As she opened the door to the bookshop a feeling of calmness washed over her, there really was something about this little place that made her feel connected with her mother and her heritage. In that moment she made the decision, she was going to make a success of the little bookshop. She felt confident and she was determined to make this a success.

As Prue lined up the cleaning products on the counter there was a knock on the open door. She turned to see an older man stood there with a toolbox, it was Walter the local electrician. He had worked for her grandmother a handful of times and so Prue trusted him to look at the shop's electrics.

'Thank you for coming here, Walter.' Prue smiled at him and made her way to the door to shake his hand.

'Your grandmother would not be happy.' He grunted as he let go of her hand and looked around at the gloomy shop.

'Why not?' Prue was intrigued, she felt nothing but happiness from this little shop, why would her grandmother be unhappy?

'This was your mother's, this shop. Nothing good ever came from it.' Before explaining any further, Walter placed his toolbox on the floor and began to root around in it for the correct tools. His body language clearly stated that the conversation was over and as much as Prue wanted to ask more questions she didn't want to risk being electrocuted when she turned the lights on.

They both worked in silence, Walter fixed the fuse box whilst Prue dusted and cleaned every surface she could. Her mind was buzzing with Walter's words, what had he meant when he had said that nothing good had ever come from this bookshop?

'All done!' Walter announced and with a flick of a switch the huge brass chandelier above lit up, casting light throughout the room. Prue looked around in awe as she took in the vibrant colours of all the books on the shelves. It was beautiful. With the flick of another switch wall lights in the shape of old fashioned torches lit up. It was as though you had just stepped foot into an 18th century library. Prue felt a fizz of excitement as she stood on the balcony looking down at her new venture.

'Thank you, Walter!' Prue called as she climbed down the ladder back to the shop floor.

'You're welcome, miss. Good luck, the village folk won't be happy about this.' Walter picked up his toolbox and turned on his heel to leave the building.

'What do you mean?' Prue called after him, running to the door to catch up with him.

'I'll send you my invoice.' He called back, without even turning back to look at her.

Prue shut the door behind him and sunk down to the floor. Despair filled her body as she tried to un-tangle the mass of jumbled thoughts whizzing around her head. She wanted to immerse herself into village life and be respected by the villagers and yet here she was, seemingly about to embark on a venture that would only anger them more. This place deserved to be shared though, it really was a treasure trove of books and a reader's dream. Not to mention the endless memories that were trapped inside of these four walls. With a new resolve, Prue stood up and picked up her feather duster. She would show the villagers that she was here to stay and unlike her grandmother she wanted to be an integral part of their daily life, not just there to benefit from them paying their rent.

With a renewed sense of determination, Prue began to dust the books behind the counter, these were the older and rarer editions. From her experiences in auction houses Prue recognised the value of these books immediately. However, there was one particular book that stood out from the others. It wasn't old, nor did it look special in anyway. With her curiosity piqued Prue put her duster down and pulled the book from the shelf. It was leather bound like the others, however where the others had their colours faded this one was still a vibrant red. It felt heavy in Prue's hands as she turned it over to see the cover. The cover had a beautiful gold gilded dragonfly on the front, similar to the one on the Clemonte crest. Prue made her way over to the leather chair, which had now be cleaned and buffed to within an inch of its life. She sat down and pulled her legs up underneath her, snuggling into the warm embrace of the chair. As she opened the cover to the book Prue felt her heart skip a beat.

She read the two lines over and over.

This diary belongs to:

Dorothy Clemonte

It was her mother's diary. Prue wondered whether this diary would tell her why the villagers were so against the bookshop and the Clemonte family. Her hands trembled as she turned the next page to see her mother's handwriting scrawled across it. Prue paused before she began reading, it didn't feel quite right. Her mother had obviously hidden the diary for a reason. Shouldn't she respect that and leave her mother's thoughts and secrets alone? With a sigh, Prue put the diary in her bag, it would be safer back at the manor. Prue didn't know whether to read it or to leave it be. On the one hand she was eager to know what was inside it but she also knew that she should respect her mother's privacy. With a sigh she stood up from the chair and went to busy herself cleaning, it would do no good to sit and mull things over all afternoon.

By the time the sun had set Prue had cleaned every inch of the little bookshop. If the village had a taxi service she would have treated herself to a ride home, however it didn't and so she was forced to walk. The hills felt endless and higher than Mount Everest. By the time she reached the front door to the manor, every part of her ached and her forehead glistened with a fresh layer of sweat. There was nothing that Prue wanted more than a long soak in a hot bath and so that was exactly what she did.

The tub was filled almost to the top with lavender scented bubbles bobbing around on the surface. Prue sighed in relief as she submerged herself in the water. It wasn't until she relaxed and allowed her mind to wander that she remembered she had her mother's diary sat at the bottom of her bag where she had discarded it in the hallway. Prue's fingers itched to grab the diary and start reading it but she knew it would be wrong. With a sigh, she promised herself that she would respect her mother's privacy and leave the diary alone. At least for now.

CHAPTER SIX

The following day, Prue woke feeling much happier. Although the little bookshop was clean and tidy it still needed a few finishing touches to make it perfect for its grand reopening. Prue was planning on visiting the shop today to make a list of things she needed, before travelling to one of the bigger towns tomorrow to buy everything on her list. Yesterday, Prue had discovered a door at the back of the shop which led into a tiny kitchenette, just big enough for one person to move around comfortably. The kitchenette had needed a good scrub but once the layer of dust had been removed it looked fairly functional, it was only missing one fundamental appliance - a coffee machine. In addition to a coffee machine there were a few other little things that Prue wanted to purchase to make the bookshop feel even cosier. She wanted a throw to drape over the leather chair, a couple of stools to allow others to sit and flick through a book and the final thing on Prue's list was a globe. As a child she remembered accompanying her grandmother on a handful of shopping trips and she would always beg to go into the bookshop that had a globe in the middle of the shop. She would run straight to it and stare in awe at all the places in the world that she was yet to discover. Prue's vision for the bookshop was to turn it into a little haven for readers and people who just wanted to nip in and relax.

Prue flourished when she had a task at hand and having a task that meant so much to her filled her with joy. She may not have many memories of her mother but she would make sure her legacy was a success. Prue would use the bookshop to weave her way into the heart of the village. She hadn't quite worked out how she was going to achieve it, but she would. In theory, it was a brilliant plan.

With a bounce in her step, Prue got ready for the day. Knowing that she wouldn't be scrubbing every surface in sight Prue took her favourite dress down from her wardrobe. It was a black and white polkadot tea dress that was cut just above the knee. She curled her hair and applied some bright red lipstick. Now she felt ready to face the day. Prue slipped on her black heels and picked up her bag, she was going to drive to the shop today, there was no way she would survive a second day of walking back up that hill.

The drive into the village was serene, it was yet again another beautiful day outside. Prue felt like a weight had been lifted from her shoulders after deciding not to read her mother's diary. The book was now stashed away in her desk drawer at home. She still felt a pull to open it up and discover all of her mother's hidden secrets but she knew what a betrayal it would be. Still, it was difficult to know that so many memories lay unread and just waiting for Prue to pick the book up and start reading. Prue Clemonte enjoyed everything to do with history, after all she had worked at an auction house. One of Prue's favourite things about her job was picking up an item and imagining its history and what it had seen. Each item held memories of someone's lifetime and to Prue that meant a lot.

Prue forced herself to focus on the present as she parked the car and made a mental note to start thinking about buying a new car, something smaller and easier to park. Her heart skipped a beat as she approached the little bookshop and remembered that it was all hers. The sign above the door was just about visible in the sun today, despite the paint having mostly chipped off. From what Prue could still read it looked as though it was once called *The Vintage Bookshop of Memories*. The name was befitting, it was romantic and yet described the place so perfectly.

She would ensure that the sign was restored to its original glory.

An hour later Prue's list had grown substantially and she was beginning to wonder how she would ever have the shop ready to open again. Just as she was giving up hope there was a knock at the door. Prue jumped and dropped both her notepad and pen. She was thankful that the knock hadn't been two minutes earlier when she was prancing around the shop singing ABBA tunes at the top of her voice. Prue could never resist ABBA.

'Hello?' She called, swinging the door open to see a rather good looking man on the other side who was beaming back at her.

'Prue Clemonte?' He asked, his dark eyes were boring into hers. Prue stood there taking in his appearance from his jet black hair, chiseled jaw covered in a smattering of stubble and his crisp suit. He was very good looking.

'Hello?' His voice echoed throughout the shop, making Prue jump again.

'How can I help you?' Prue asked, trying to regain her composure and cover the fact that she had just been standing there like an idiot admiring his good looks for the past god knows how long.

'My name's Elliot Harrington. I work with Mr Adley.' Of course he was here on business, a good looking man like him would never just come knocking on her door.

'Please, Mr Harrington, come in.' Prue moved to the side to allow the man through the door.

'Call me Elliot, please.' Prue watched as Elliot stepped into the shop and looked around in awe at the place. She was glad she wasn't the only one who was overwhelmed by the beauty of the bookshop.

'How can I help you, Elliot?' Prue retrieved her notepad and pen from the floor and walked over to the counter whilst Elliot averted his eyes from his surroundings and re-focused on her.

'Mr Adley has been going through all the paperwork and he found a letter addressed to you.' He explained, pulling a battered looking envelope from his pocket. Prue took it from him and turned it over in her hands, the front simply said 'Prudence' and it looked to be in her mother's handwriting.

'Thank you for delivering this, Elliot.' Prue smiled, she was trying to be polite but all she wanted was to sit down in the comfy chair and read this letter, with nobody around to disturb her.

'You're welcome miss. Is it true that this place is haunted?'

'Haunted?' Prue asked. She had known something had happened but the last thing she had expected was for it to be haunted.

'It's probably nothing but as a child we were always told that it was haunted. Perhaps it was just to stop kids from breaking in.' He explained, his eyes glancing nervously around the shop. Prue wondered what had happened within these four-walls that meant her grandmother had to make up stories about the shop being haunted.

'Not that I'm aware of. I believe my mother opened the shop, although I'm not sure why it shut. I would imagine that the villagers didn't much like her being amongst them.' Prue hadn't meant to have such a bitter edge to her tone but she couldn't help it. Her family had helped the villagers for years, fairly renting land to them that they otherwise couldn't have afforded. Yet all the people saw was them pretending to be Lords of the Manor and not caring about their subjects. They couldn't have been further from the truth. All Prue wanted was to allow everyone to continue living their life, she just wanted to be able to live happily beside them.

'Ah. Yes, I don't think you're the village favourite if I'm completely honest.' Elliot replied with an almost sheepish look on his face.

'I'm aware.' Prue rolled her eyes and tried to fight the memories from the other morning in the cafe. That was not an experience she wished to relive.

'I best be off. See you around.' Elliot smiled at her before letting himself out of the shop.

Prue stared after him feeling somewhat confused. She had only been home for a week and yet she had already adjusted to a life of isolation. Meeting Elliot today had reminded her how much she enjoyed being around others and talking to them. It also helped that he was very good looking.

With a jolt Prue remembered what she was holding in her hand. A letter from her mother. She made her way over to the leather chair and sat down, with trembling hands she undid the envelope and slid a single piece of paper out. The note had been written on a cream piece of paper with a boarder of vintage books. The paper was almost insignificant to the words on it, however Prue knew that it was the exact sheet of paper she would have chosen for an important note. With a deep breath and a tissue to hand Prue began reading her mother's words.

My darling Prue,

As I sit and write this you're lying in your cot, only a few days old. You're the most beautiful little girl I've ever laid eyes upon.

Prue, I wanted to leave you a few clues. I'm not sure what the future holds for either of us and incase anything happens to me I want you to be able to learn who you truly are. I'm going to give this letter to Mr Adley and instruct him to only give it to you if both me and you grandmother are dead. I hope this day never comes but I have to be prepared since it's only the two of us.

Prue, you may only be a few days old but you're my world. I'm sorry I couldn't give you a proper family. I promise to do my best for you.

I'm sure you've wondered on many occasions who your father is. If you've asked me or your grandmother we won't have told you. You see it caused a few problems in the village when your father and I were together. We were very different people and we couldn't be together.

He doesn't know about you and I'm sorry about that. It's how it had to be.

I'm worried who may see this letter and so I cannot write his name. I can leave you a clue though.

Look for him in my diary, you'll find it in the bookshop.

All my love,

Mum

P.S If you're anything like me you'll be itching to read the diary. Read it if you want to. By the time you find out who your father is there'll be no more secrets.
xxx

Her father. Prue had never thought much about her father. As a child she spent most of the academic year at boarding school and whilst some of the girls spoke of their fathers they were all alone at school. Perhaps now was the time to think about her father. Prue was suddenly hit by a revelation, her father could be alive. If he was then perhaps she didn't have to do this alone, she didn't have to face the village wrath with nobody by her side. There was another side of her that felt as though she were betraying both her mother and grandmother, they had kept him a secret from her for a reason. Did she really want to delve into the unknown when she was happy enough getting by on her own? A part of her wanted to know what the secrets were that her mother alluded to, however another part of her just wanted to ignore it all. Life wasn't perfect but Prue didn't want to open up a whole box of secrets and complicate things even more. Her mind wandered to where the diary was hidden away in her drawer, it would be so easy to just pick it up and start reading.

CHAPTER SEVEN

After reading the letter Prue had gone straight home to the manor. She wanted to completely shut herself away from the outside world and wallow in her loneliness. As she drove out of the village she saw all the glares and hateful glances that each person sent her way. Prue wanted to endure the storm and show the village that she was here for good and for their benefit but there was only so much hate she could cope with. She got home and made herself a cup of tea, with tears pouring down her cheeks, before venturing into the one room in the house that sent a chill down her spine. Her mother's room. Despite the eeriness of it, Prue felt a pull towards the room and the memories that it held, of one of the most important people in her life.

The room was exactly how her mother had left it on the day she died, although the medical equipment had since been removed. Dorothy had been unwell her entire life and over the years her health had deteriorated and so Prue's grandmother had hired a live-in nurse, until the day she had to go into hospital. The room was as if time had stood still, her blusher brush stood on the make up table with the compact powder left open, collecting dust. The pale pink curtains were tied back in little bows, just how her mother had liked them. Every little piece of that room was exactly how she had left it on that fateful day. Prue didn't remember that day but her grandmother had told her what had happened. It had been a dull September day, the winds were whipping up and a storm was forecast for that evening. Everyone was being warned to stay indoors and keep safe. Her mother's heart was struggling more and more with every breath she took and so they had taken the decision to call an ambulance. Prue had been left behind with her nanny, with the promise that they would be home soon. Sometimes Prue dreamed of that night as the wind howled outside and she waited for her mother and grandmother to return home. She was unsure how much was based on her own memories and how much was based on what she had been told. Either way, the empty feeling that it left her with would always haunt Prue.

Prue didn't really know how to feel about her mother's death. Of course she was sad and she missed her and yet she had been so young that she didn't remember much about her mother. It was a strange thing to grieve for someone that you didn't know and yet she didn't feel that way about her father. Prue had always yearned for a mother-figure in her life. Her grandmother ensured that she never went without and dropped her off at boarding school at the beginning of each new term but other than that she had no parental figures in her life, other than the endless nannies. That was okay though, after all it had shaped her into the woman she was today.

As Prue wandered around her mother's room she tried to make a decision. Did she search for the father that she felt no connection to or did she just carry on life as normal? It felt like such a big decision for just one person to make. She walked over to the window and watched as the sun set over the village. As Prue searched within herself she knew that being accepted by the villagers was more important to her than being accepted by her father. A thought crossed her mind though, her mother had dropped a hint about the village and her father being connected. Her mind was jumbled with chaotic thoughts, all merging into one another. With a sigh, Prue made a decision. The information about her father was in that diary, it wasn't going anywhere. For now Prue had to create a life for herself and find her place in the village before she could go searching for another part of her. Her mother had mentioned there being secrets and so Prue had to find these out before she delved into the diary. Prue went to get the diary from her drawer and placed it on her mother's bed. It would be there for whenever she was ready.

The evening was long and when Prue did fall asleep she had a restless sleep filled with dreams of the night her mother died. Prue was worried about whether or not she had made the right decision. Could turning your back on your own flesh and blood ever be considered the right decision? The birds sang outside Prue's window alerting her to the fact that it was morning. As much as Prue wanted to hide under the duvet and pretend the world outside didn't exist she knew she had to keep forging ahead. One day at a time.

Prue managed a couple of hours of sleep, in the early hours of the morning, when she woke she knew she had to push herself to keep going, to live her life as if nothing out of the ordinary was going on. Despite yesterday's revelations she would stick to her original plans and make a start on buying the items on her list for the shop. As she climbed out of bed her gaze wandered to her mother's bedroom door which was just across the hallway. A little peek would be all it took and then she would know her full heritage. She shook her head and turned her attention back to the task at hand, today was not the day to delve into her DNA.

After a quick shower Prue felt a little more alert and ready to face the day. Perhaps she would call one of her friends in Brighton for a chat tonight, it would do her good to talk things through with someone. There's only so much one person can have whizzing around their head. Prue took a burgundy tea dress from her wardrobe and settled on just pinning her hair back into a bun. She didn't feel much like making an effort today. Sometimes she wished she was the kind of girl that could just grab a pair of jeans and a jumper, but she wasn't. She didn't even own a pair of jeans.

Usually, Prue was the kind of person who loved shopping. She enjoyed the buzz of the crowds and the frenzied look on everyone's face as they hunted down pieces to buy. However, today the people annoyed her and everyone just seemed to be in her way. Slowly, she was ticking things off of her list but it involved lots of trips back to the car to deposit bags. Sometimes being on her own was difficult and she yearned to have someone by her side, if only to carry a few bags.

If Prue was honest with herself she knew that part of the reason she couldn't concentrate was because her mind was still reeling from her mother's revelation. It was ridiculous, not once had Prue ever wanted to know who her father was and yet here she was, presented with the possibility of a name and it had completely thrown her.

Prue took a deep breath after dropping another load of bags off at the car. She had to push these thoughts to the back of her mind and concentrate on today. Today was for buying pieces for the shop to make it hers, it wasn't a day to focus on the past. She had to make a success of the bookshop. That was far more important than finding out a name, wasn't it?

CHAPTER EIGHT

Once Prue stopped focusing on her parentage she found that she had a rather productive day. After ticking off everything on her list Prue had made the decision to stop off at one of the local car garages and she was now the proud owner of a vintage Mini. She had stared at the sparkling new cars with their air conditioning and bluetooth and willed herself to fall in love with one, but then she spotted the old green Mini and she knew at once nothing else on the forecourt would compare. The Mini had leather seats that would stick to her legs in the summer and the gear stick looked ancient. Despite this, Prue had fallen in love with the memories that the Mini held. She thought about all the people that had driven it, all the trips that it had made and all the laughs that it had witnessed. Those memories were what stole her heart and now there the Mini was, sat proudly beside Prue's vintage Bentley. Every time Prue glanced out of the window she felt a little flutter of excitement knowing that those two cars were all hers.

She had glanced one more time at the cars before going to bed and the following morning the first thing she did was run to front door to check they were still there. It wasn't a dream. Who needed parents when vintage cars existed? Prue chuckled to herself at her dark sense of humour, she had to laugh or else she might cry over her situation. She shook her head and went about getting herself ready for the day. The bags of shopping that she bought yesterday were waiting to be unpacked at the shop. Prue opted for a cream tea-dress, nipped in at the waist and covered in bumble bees, complete with a sweet Peter Pan collar. It was a little twee for her but she adored it. She threw a grey cardigan around her shoulders and pulled on some brogues. She was ready to go and put her own stamp on *The Vintage Bookshop of Memories*.

A vintage Mini had been a great idea, although in hindsight she had done rather a lot of shopping yesterday. Somehow, she managed to wedge each and every bag into the car and soon she was pootling along through the village enjoying every second of driving her new car. Her drive through the village was rather serene this morning, nobody recognised her in her new car and so she avoided the hateful glares as she drove through the main street. With ease, Prue parked the car and began to make the numerous trips to the bookshop with all of her bags.

'Can I help?' A voice called, making her jump and hit her head on the boot of her car. With a hand clinging to her now pounding head Prue turned around to see who was offering to help her. Surely nobody in this village would help her? Prue was surprised to see Elliot, the man who had delivered her mother's letter, standing behind her trying not to laugh. He was dressed just as smartly today with a black fitted suit, a white shirt and an emerald coloured tie which almost sparkled in the early morning sunlight. He may have been laughing at her but that didn't stop him from being any less attractive, which made it difficult for Prue to glare back at him.

'Sorry, I didn't mean to make you jump.' He chuckled, reaching forward to pick up a handful of bags. Despite his annoying overly-happy-manner Prue was grateful for some help.

'Lucky you work for Mr Adley so when I sue you you'll be able to get employee's discount.' Prue watched as a look of horror flickered across Elliot's face, her grave tone had obviously worked.

'I'm sorry, I was only trying to help. Why don't I treat you to lunch later to show you just how sorry I am?' His smile had quickly returned as he shrugged off her attempt at teasing him.

'Are you sure you want to be seen out with me? I'm village enemy number one.' As much as Prue wanted to integrate herself into village life she didn't want to risk putting anyone else in the path of the village's wrath.

'I'm sure I can handle it.' He shrugged looking blasé, and shooting Prue a cheeky smile so that she almost dropped the bag she was holding.

After another trip to and from the car Elliot left, promising to see Prue again at lunchtime. Prue was left staring after him wondering what had just happened. She had planned for a quiet day putting the final touches to her beloved bookshop and yet here she was with lunch plans. She felt almost nervous at the prospect of having lunch with Elliot but she was unsure whether it was because she was attracted to him or whether it was because of the village's reaction. Prue knew it would do no good to spend the morning worrying over it and so she took off her cardigan and began to unbox the mountain of items she had bought.

Perhaps she had gone a little overboard with her shopping but she had wanted to put her own mark on the bookshop, whilst honouring its priceless memories. Prue draped a beautiful tweed blanket over the back of the leather chair, it was in beautiful shades of grey and pale yellow. It made the old comfortable chair look even more inviting and invoked thoughts of curling up on it with a good book. As Prue delved into another bag she pulled out some vintage bunting. The little triangles were each made from offcuts of vintage clothes. When Prue saw them she knew that she had to have them, she was going to string them on the balcony railings.

As the clock struck midday, Prue took a step back and admired the changes that her finishing touches had brought about. The shop was starting to reflect her love for vintage things. In one of the antique shops she had come across lots of old teddy bears and so she had bought them to place around the shelves in the small area of the shop that was dedicated to children's books. Somehow the magic that her mother had created inside this little bookshop was magnified by all of the little touches that Prue had added. In the middle of the shop was a huge round mahogany table which Prue had now furnished with a beautiful lace table cloth. She was going to change the table's theme each week. This week she had opted to honour the war and would leave it that way until the shop opened. The table was scattered with fiction and non-fiction war books and poppies were scattered around the table. She hoped that the villagers might provide pictures of local soldiers that she could also display on the table. Prue knew she was getting a little ahead of herself but she meant it, she wanted the bookshop to be a part of the community, even if she couldn't be.

Before Prue's mind could wander any further there was a knock at the door and Elliot let himself in.

'Oh wow, it looks amazing.' Prue watched in delight as Elliot spun around taking everything in. She watched as his eyes fell upon a retro suitcase filled with books. Prue had found the bag of books filling one of the little cupboards in the back kitchen. After some investigating she discovered that each book had an imperfection. Instead of throwing them away she decided to make a feature of it and offer them at a discounted price. Well if she was honest she had seen the suitcase, fallen in love with it and needed to justify buying it.

'Do you still think it's haunted?' Prue asked, as she left Elliot staring in awe as she ran to grab her cardigan and handbag. It was warm in the shop but she suspected the late-April breeze outside would be chilly, not to mention the icy glares the majority of the village would be giving her.

'No I think you might have scared the ghouls away.' Elliot

chuckled as he spun back round to see her coming out from the kitchenette. Prue watched as the breath caught in his throat and his eyes bore into hers. Perhaps this lunch wasn't just a way to say sorry. With that in mind, Prue felt a blush rise in her cheeks.

'You ready?' He asked, clearing his throat and edging towards the door. The atmosphere inside the shop had changed, its usual laidback feeling was almost electric, Prue could feel her skin fizzling.

'Let's go.' She smiled, wanting to get out into the fresh air and shake this feeling. She wasn't against a relationship right now, she just had lots to think about and she suspected Elliot Harrington would complicate things.

They walked together through the church yard towards the village, leaving just enough space between them to ensure their hands didn't accidentally brush against each other as they walked.

'So Elliot Harrington, what's your story?' Prue wanted to know more about the brave man stood next to her, who was accompanying her into the lion's den.

'Well Miss Clemonte I'm a good honest country boy. Grew up with my parents and two brothers on one of the local farms. Then I did the unforgivable thing and decided I didn't want to be a farmer, I wanted to go to law school. My father refused to speak to me during my entire time at university, it's only since I came back from university that he's finally started saying hello to me again. I'm now a trainee solicitor at Mr Adley's firm and I live in one of the cottages on the outskirts of the village.'

'Do you think your relationship with your dad will improve?' Prue asked, trying to keep her voice level, she didn't want to give away the fact that she fancied Elliot.

'We'll see. I don't have high hopes, he's very stuck in his ways. It doesn't help that both of my brothers are working on the farm.

I'm therefore the black sheep of my family, no pun intended.' Prue chuckled at Elliot's terrible joke. Behind the facade there was a sadness in his eyes, perhaps he longed for the same relationship with his father that his brothers had.

'What about you Miss Clemonte, what's your story?' In a flash the sadness in Elliot's eyes had been replaced with a smile as he opened the churchyard gate, which led them to the main road through the village.

'Well Mr Harrington, I'm the current Lady of the Manor. I suppose I didn't really get the chance to decide whether or not I wanted to go into the family business, I just inherited it.' Saying it out loud made Prue realise why she was so excited about the bookshop, this was something she wanted, whereas the responsibility of the estate was not something she wanted.

'And what would you have chosen to do?' Elliot asked with genuine interest on his face as he took her arm and steered her towards the village pub. Her arm tingled where he had touched her.

'Before my grandmother's death I was working in Brighton at an auction house, I valued the items.'

Prue kept her answer short as they were just about to walk into the pub and the last thing she wanted was to draw any attention to herself. As the door swung open and they walked in every pair of eyes in there turned to look at them. Prue watched as anger crossed the faces of everyone in the building.

'She's not welcome in here.' The man behind the bar growled at them, nodding his head towards Prue, incase anyone didn't know who he was talking about.

'Come on Harry, we just want some lunch. Prue lives in this village too. In fact she owns this pub so surely that should give her rights?' Prue wanted the ground to open up and swallow her. She appreciated Elliot trying to fight her corner but she really didn't want any confrontation.

'Well she can have the pub if she wants, not that anyone would drink here.' The barman, Harry, called back through gritted teeth.

'I don't want the pub. Come on Elliot.' Prue pulled Elliot back onto the street outside, she was absolutely mortified.

'This behaviour is ridiculous. The village's feud was between your grandmother and the villagers, not you.'

'Elliot, do you know what the feud was about?'

'I'm not sure, I was too young to remember when it all happened. My father would probably know.'

Just as Elliot finished his sentence a bellowing voice came from the other side of the road.

'Elliot Harrington, what do you think you're doing?'

Both Prue and Elliot turned towards the voice. It was the same man that had been shouting at Prue in the cafe earlier in the week.

'Good afternoon, father!' Elliot called back, a huge grin on his face. Prue's face completely drained of colour, how could charming Elliot be the son of such a brute?

'Here's my card, give me a text and I'll let you know if I find anything out.' He shot Prue a quick wink before running across the road to where his father, stood almost glowing with anger. Prue didn't want to overhear their conversation and so she quickly made her way back to the bookshop. She had the kitchenette to sort out this afternoon. With a lot of discipline she stopped her mind from wandering and focused on washing the vintage tea cups she had bought yesterday and placing them carefully on the shelves. The little kitchen could do with a revamp at some point with its pale pink cupboards and wooden worktop, it was all bit too girly for Prue but it had suited her mother. Perhaps for that reason alone she would keep the kitchenette the way it was, as a little reminder that her mother was by her side.

CHAPTER NINE

Thankfully, Prue had bought enough vintage tea cups to keep her busy all afternoon. Actually, she'd bought enough vintage tea cups to provide each member of the village with a cup of tea. Not that anyone would be coming to her for a sit down, a cup of tea and a natter. That evening, as Prue made her way back to the manor, she was grateful to have her new car so that none of the villagers recognised her, for now at least. She knew she would have to confront everyone at some point, she couldn't continue to live like this. However, the idea of confronting the entire village made her very nervous, she would put it off for as long as possible.

Prue was beginning to see the appeal of the Clemonte manor. It was big and foreboding but it was home. Once those wrought iron gates were shut behind her she felt safe inside her own little haven. The driveway was lined with rose trees on either side and in summer they would look and smell divine. This was her home and no matter how hostile the people were she wouldn't be moved. As she climbed out of her car and walked up to the front door Prue took a moment to really appreciate her surroundings. The manor had a substantial amount of land surrounding it with an acre of manicured lawn out the back and formal gardens on either side of the driveway. Beyond the gardens were wild meadows rolling down towards the village. It was absolutely breathtaking and thanks to their lovely gardener, who lived on the edge of the estate, Prue didn't have to worry about a thing. Prue let out a sigh as she looked towards the village, it looked so picturesque and inviting. To an outsider it would look like the perfect place to live, in reality it would only be perfect if the population moved. Prue sighed, why couldn't they just be nice to her?

Sometimes the silence in the manor was deafening. Prue was in need of a chat and so she made herself a gin fizz in a crystal tumbler and went to sit outside on the patio to call her friend, Katie. Prue and Katie had been at university together and then opted to move to a house share together. They had shared a lot of happy moments living life to the full in Brighton. Although Prue was loving being home she missed having people around her. She missed the socialising and knowing that wherever she went in town there would always be someone to chat to. Here, there was nobody, unless you counted Elliot but Prue doubted she would hear from him again. At some point that afternoon she had bravely pulled out her phone and given him a quick text. That way he had her number and so he could contact her if he wanted to.

As the sun set in the distance Prue listened to Katie tell her about how beautiful Brighton was looking from their balcony. She told Prue all about the new housemate who had moved in, a rather good looking young man. He had only moved in three days ago and Katie already had a date with him. A wave of sadness came over Prue as she realised that her old life was continuing without her, nobody's life had changed that much without her there. Meanwhile she was here trying to win over an entire village to stop them from glaring at her and shunning her from all public spaces. Somehow it didn't seem fair that she was in this situation all because of which family she had been born into. She hadn't asked for any of this.

After putting the phone down Prue felt a sense of loneliness. She was home, the place where she should feel the most content, instead here she was worrying about bumping into one of the villagers. There was also a part of her that was somewhat concerned about her safety. Who knew what lengths the people of

Ivy Hatch would go to? Prue only wished she knew what she and her family had done to upset them. Perhaps now was the right time to start reading her mother's diary. Would there ever be a right time?

With a sigh Prue stood up and decided to make herself a huge bowl of pasta, that would help. She couldn't just go and read her mother's diary on a whim, this had to be a well thought-out decision. Instead, she would eat her feelings, it usually helped improve her mood. Prue made her way into the house through the French doors and into the kitchen. The kitchen had been renovated whilst Prue was away at University. The wooden floor was buffed and polished to within an inch of its life and reflected the sun that poured in from the back wall, which boasted floor to ceiling windows looking out on the manicured lawn. The kitchen cabinets were navy with chrome handles and a wooden worktop. She had to admit the interior designer that her grandmother had hired had taste. Prue grabbed some pasta from the pantry and made her way over towards the range. As she switched the range on and waited for the water to boil she felt her phone vibrate from the pocket in her dress. She pulled it out expecting to see a picture from Katie of her new love interest, however to Prue's surprise Elliot's name flashed up on her screen. Her heart began to race as she unlocked her phone to read his message.

Dear Prue,

I think I might have started to unravel the mystery as to why the villagers dislike your family. It's too much to put into a text so why don't you come over for dinner tomorrow, around 7? Elliot x

Prue had to laugh at the formal tone of his text but it was also a distraction from the butterflies that were swarming in the pit of her stomach. Dinner with Elliot Harrington? Prue wanted to know why she was so disliked but was getting close to Elliot the best way to go about it? She liked him, lots, but she didn't want to get him into trouble with the village. It was all so confusing. At least this way she didn't have to delve into her mother's diary, yet.

As the water began to boil Prue stared at it, wondering what to do. On one hand she liked Elliot and wanted to know what he had found out. However, she also knew that if he was seen associating himself with her then he would be outcast from village life. He had invited her though and he did know her history with Ivy Hatch and its occupants. With a sigh Prue grabbed her phone and text Elliot back saying she looked forward to seeing him tomorrow evening. Within seconds his reply came with his address. Perhaps it was selfish of her to drag him into her family's mess but sometimes you had to be a little selfish in life to get what you wanted.

CHAPTER TEN

The following day Prue spent most of her time worrying about dinner with Elliot. She didn't know what to wear, how to act, should she bring dessert? What about a bottle of wine? With an exasperated sigh Prue turned her attention back to her wardrobe. Eventually she settled on a white blouse with capped sleeves and an A-line Burgundy skirt, which was cut just above her knee. It was casual and yet looked like she had put some thought into it. Prue had never had this problem before, at university and during her time living in Brighton her relationships had often come about through Tinder, meaning that she didn't have the awkward 'is this or isn't this a date?' Although she knew her dinner with Elliot was not a date, he just had some information to give her. Nevertheless he was going to a lot of effort cooking for her and so she wanted to at least make some effort in return. Well, that's what she was telling herself anyway. She was definitely not making the effort because she fancied him.

With a quick glance in the mirror Prue pinned back her curls and reapplied some red lipstick. She was ready. Although Elliot's cottage was only on the outskirts of the village Prue still opted to drive there. The hills that she would have to walk up on her way home made the short walk a lot less inviting.

The drive down to the village was peaceful and thankfully there was nobody around to stare at Prue. After her treatment from the villagers yesterday Prue had opted to stay away from the bookshop today. It was almost ready to open but she couldn't do that until she had won over the village. Instead she had spent the day in the library at the manor, curled up on one of the worn sofas losing herself in endless books. She had to keep her brain busy or else she risked being overwhelmed with everything that was going on. Not to mention the niggling voice in the back of her head which was encouraging her to read her mother's diary and find out who her father was.

Before Prue's mind could run away with itself she pulled up outside Elliot's cottage and a small gasp escaped her. It was absolutely gorgeous. Prue had passed this cottage many times and she knew that during summer the front was covered in wisteria with lavender growing on either side of the cobbled path that led to the front door. The sash windows had sage green shutters on either side and the door was painted to match them. Prue could barely believe how quaint and homely this little cottage appeared. She was use to either living in the manor or dank house shares in Brighton. It was like she had just stepped into an interior design magazine.

'Prue! Just in time.' Elliot swung the door open with a huge grin on his face that Prue couldn't help but return. Her heels clicked on the cobbled path as she made her way to the front door.

'Thank you for this Elliot, I know you're risking your reputation inviting me into your home!' Prue tried to keep her voice light and her words teasing but beneath it she knew the truth.

'You better come in quickly before the lynch mob see you. My thatched roof won't stand up to their torches.' Prue laughed, there was something about Elliot that made her relax when she was around him. Perhaps it was the way he didn't take anything seriously, or the way she felt safe in his presence. Whatever it was she enjoyed being around him and that was dangerous for both of them.

As Prue followed Elliot into the little cottage she found herself speechless. It was as beautiful on the inside as it was on the outside, much like it's owner. The interior was in-keeping with the age of the cottage and the colours were neutral with the odd splash of sage.

'It's beautiful, isn't it? Your grandmother had the place refurbished just before I moved in.' Elliot had a look of pride on his face as he showed her around.

'Wait, do I own this cottage?' Prue was still trying to get her head around just how much of the village she owned.

'Prue, you do realise you own every house and every business in the village, besides from the church?'

Elliot's voice resounded throughout the small space as Prue tried to process what he had just said. Prue had grown up knowing that the family owned the surrounding farms and the majority of the property in the village, she had never known that they owned the whole village.

'I own the whole village?' Prue asked, she was beginning to realise why the villagers hated her with such a passion. She also should have paid more attention to Mr Adley during her meeting with him.

'You do but I don't believe that's why everyone dislikes you, well, not quite. Come, sit down and I'll dish up dinner and tell you what I found out.'

Prue followed Elliot into a little alcove, which housed an oak table with a bench either side and in the middle stood a vase filled with tulips.

'My mother pops in and gives the place a quick once over every now and then. She also drops me off some meals and so whilst I'd love to take credit for our dinner, it was actually my mother's hard work that went into it. You see to my father I'm an outcast, to my mother I'm still her son. My father doesn't know about her visits and we like it that way.'

Prue felt a pang of sadness for Elliot, he had followed his heart and yet he was being punished for that. Despite her grandmother's strange ways she had always encouraged Prue to fulfil her dreams and follow her heart. That was how Prue had ended up in Brighton, following her heart to the hustle and bustle of a city. She always knew she had a home to come back to and here she was. Unlike Elliot though she didn't have the family.

Silently Prue watched from her seat at the table as Elliot bustled around the small kitchen and plated up their dinner. It smelled amazing. With just herself to cook for more often than not Prue ended up with a toasted cheese sandwich for dinner, if she was feeling adventurous she might add some roasted tomatoes.

'Dinner is served!' Elliot announced as he placed her plate in-front of her with a flourish. It was lasagna and it looked and smelt amazing.

'Dad insists on meat and two veg for dinner and so mum uses me to try out any new recipes she's come across.' Elliot explained as he took the seat opposite her and poured them both a glass of wine from the bottle that Prue had brought with her.

It was good, really good. Much better than anything her grandmother had ever cooked. Elizabeth Clemonte had been brought up by nannies and had a house full of servants to order around and so she had rarely had to do anything for herself. By the time Prue was born the villagers had revolted and the Clemontes had few servants. Prue refocused on the meal in-front of her and looked up to meet Elliot's eye, it was time he told her what was going on.

'Okay. Before I start I think you should take a big sip of your wine because you're not going to like what I'm about to tell you.'

A knot formed in Prue's stomach and she put her fork down and took a swig of alcohol.

'I tried asking my dad but he was useless and so when my mum popped round to give the place a little tidy I made sure I was working from home. I sat my mum down, plied her with tea and asked her a few questions about your family.' Elliot stopped to take a sip from his wine and Prue took the chance to take another gulp from hers. A part of her wasn't sure whether she wanted to hear what he had to say but she knew she had to. She had to know the truth.

'My mum once worked at the manor, even I didn't know this. Apparently after everything happened my dad told her she had to quit and they never spoke of it again. Are you okay Prue?' Elliot stopped as he noticed Prue's rapid breathing and sweaty palms.

'I'm fine. Just worried about what you're going to say and how I'm going to fix things.' She tried hard to keep the trembling out of her voice and stop the tears from falling.

'Prue your family may have done something wrong but in my eyes what the villagers did was worse. We can fix this.'

Prue was even more confused now, what could the villagers have done that caused them to hate her so much? Elliot leant across the table and took a hold of one of her hands. Normally Prue would have felt the blush rise in her cheeks and the tingle in her fingers as his hand touched hers but for now she was too focused on what he had to say.

'Prue, do you know your father?' Prue couldn't speak and so she just shook her head.

'According to my mother your father was a tradesman who had recently come to live in the village. He had just finished an apprenticeship and was looking for work and so he settled here. Apparently he and your mother fell in love, they met at the bookshop. Your father had quickly become one of the villagers and was accepted into their close-knit community. It was frowned upon that he should fall in love with a Clemonte and so the villagers drove him out. Leaving your poor mother heart-broken and pregnant with you. Your grandmother was angry, rightly so, and she took her anger out on the village. She bought every house and every piece of land that she didn't own and then she upped the rent.Your grandmother was clever, between her and Mr Adley they devised a way to ensure that the villager's rent accounted for every penny of profit that they make. They also ensured that they cannot break the contracts. Effectively, the villagers are all stuck paying extortionate rents.'

Prue was still trying to process what Elliot had said. She had always assumed that her father had been a horrible person and had left her mother when he discovered she was pregnant. That wasn't the case though, he had been driven away. Anger was boiling away inside of Prue. How dare the villagers interfere like that and deprive her mother of love and steal her father from her. In that moment Prue had a renewed respect for her grand-mother. Despite the woman's lack of maternal instinct she had fought to protect her family and she had declared war on those that had hurt her daughter and her grandchild.

'I think I'd like to go home now Elliot.' Prue whispered, she didn't trust herself enough not to break down into uncontrol-lable sobs.

'Would you like me to drive you home?' Prue thought about the offer for a moment. She really wanted to be on her own but with her trembling hands and erratic thoughts she wasn't sure how she would get herself home.

'Yes, please.'

Without saying another word Elliot helped her out to his car and drove her home. The silence was far from awkward. He seemed to understand that Prue was caught up inside her own head and needed the space to process what he had just told her.

'Thank you for this evening.' Despite everything Prue would never forget her manners.

'I'm sorry I upset you Prue.' Elliot leaned across the car and gave her hand a quick squeeze.

'It's not your fault Elliot, you were just the bearer of bad news. I just need some time to process everything.'

'You take your time. Would you like me to drive your car home to you tomorrow?' The offer was nice but Prue intended to leave her car outside Elliot's, after all it would give her an excuse to see him again when her head was less confused.

'I'll come pick it up tomorrow evening, hopefully I'll be a little more coherent and we can have a drink and a chat?' Prue hoped she didn't sound too desperate but she knew she would need someone to talk to at some point. There was nobody she wanted to speak to more than Elliot right now, at least nobody who was alive.

'That's perfect. I'm working from home tomorrow so just call me or pop in whenever. Or you can call me tonight, anytime.'

The kindness in Elliot's voice made Prue want to cry. With her grandmother gone it felt like a long while since someone had last cared about her. She leaned across the car and placed a quick kiss on his cheek before climbing out. Despite her eagerness to get out of the car she still saw the blush rise on his cheeks from the kiss she had planted there.

CHAPTER ELEVEN

Once inside the manor and with the door shut behind her Prue let the tears fall from her eyes as the sobs wracked her body. She cried for her mother's pain, her grandmother's anger and most of all she cried for herself. For the father she never had the chance to know. A whole childhood that had been stolen from her because of the prejudice of an entire village. Anger boiled inside of Prue, how dare they dictate how she lived her life? Prue would make a point and she would find her father and ensure that the villagers knew about it. Nobody would tell her how to live her life.

With anger fuelling her Prue ran upstairs to her mother's bedroom, grabbed the diary and took it back to her own room. All of a sudden the adrenaline left her body and she went to sit on the window seat, which looked out over the village. With the diary grasped in her hands she looked out at all the houses below, each and every one of them had played a part in her mother's heartbreak and stopped her from growing up with a father. They deserved everything that her grandmother had done to them. In fact, they deserved more.

Taking a deep breath Prue opened her mother's diary and flicked through to the back page, her eyes scanning the pages for any clue. She wasn't sure what she had been expecting but it was immediately obvious when she eventually did stumble across her father's name. On the back page of the diary two names had been written with a love heart drawn around them. It read Dorothy Clemonte and Robert Darwin. That must be her father's name. Robert Darwin.

Prue had expected to feel something upon finding out his name but all she felt was numbness. She may now be able to put a name to her father but he was still just a stranger. Prue sat in silence staring at the page in front of her. What now? She knew his name, she knew why he left but what did she want to do now? Prue wasn't sure whether she wanted to find him or if she just wanted to forget the whole thing. Perhaps it was time for the Clemontes to leave Ivy Hatch. After all, Prue's only ties were material, there was nothing really keeping her here. Unless she considered Elliot to be a tie. She did really like him and there was something about him. If Prue was completely honest with herself she liked him more than she wanted to admit, she felt as though she could be truly happy with him. But to do that she would have to get to know him better and she suspected the entire village would be against that. Would it end the same way as it had with her mother and father?

There was so much to consider and Prue's mind was buzzing. She had two options, stay in the village and try to make it work or run away and start fresh. As she sat staring out the window she saw her two possible futures flash in front of her. She could stay here, run the little bookshop and possibly explore a relationship with Elliot. Or she could move anywhere, perhaps to a little seaside town. She could even open up her own bookshop and see whether there were any jobs at some local auction houses. The opportunities were endless but her heart was firmly in one future. This was her home, it was where her family had lived for generations, it was where all her memories lived. The moment she had set foot into the bookshop she had felt a connection with it, she had felt close to her mother. Wherever she went in the world she would never feel like that again. This village was precious to her and she had as much as a right to live here as everyone else. Actually, she had more of a right considering she owned the village.

With a new resolve Prue wiped the tears from her eyes and took a deep breath in an attempt to control her emotions. She would make a life for herself here and the villagers would have to put up with it. Perhaps she could talk to Elliot about the contracts and give them the option to leave. She didn't want to force them to stay, perhaps having some fresh blood around would be nice. And so that was decided, she would stay in the area and she would make it work.

Once Prue had made her decision she looked down at the diary in her hands, her fingers tracing the dragonfly on the cover. If she was going to stay here and be happy she had to begin to know the truth. With trembling hands she turned the page and glanced down at the writing. The diary seemed to span from her mother's eighteenth birthday to a few days before her death. With this in mind Prue flicked through the pages looking for her father's name. The rest of her mother's memories could wait until Prue was in a better frame of mind, for now she had to learn about her mother and father's relationship.

Prue found an entry that was a year and a half before her birthdate and it looked to be the day her parents met. A strange sense of excitement filled Prue, she was about to find out the answers to so many of her questions. This was where her own story started, with her parents meeting. Perhaps she should have made herself a gin fizz to accompany the reading, it was too late now though, her eyes were already scanning her mother's words.

◆ ◆ ◆

1st June 1994 -

Dear diary,

Mother has finally said I can have my own little bookshop! She's finally realised that there's nothing else I want more. Well, other than a beating heart. We've agreed that for now it's the perfect little project for me, especially while I'm in good health.

She gave me the choice to pick from some of the buildings we own in the village and I've found the perfect one. It's small but cosy and I can just see how magical it will look once I've finished. I've been sketching my ideas and sending them to the girls; they're all looking forward to coming down for the grand opening.

There's a new man in town, Robert. He's absolutely gorgeous. I've asked him to do some work on the bookshop for me and he agreed. I almost missed what he was saying because I was too busy staring into his sparkling green eyes. He has a chiselled jaw line, perfect bow shaped lips and shaggy black hair that just falls over his forehead. Diary, I think I now believe in love at first sight. Thankfully I stopped myself looking like a complete idiot. He's coming into the shop tomorrow to discuss what I want. I cannot wait!

I have to decide what to wear. Perhaps that purple maxi dress?

Until tomorrow diary...

Prue stared down at her mother's writing with fresh tears in her eyes. She had been so young, so full of the excitement for life. After all the years that her mother had suffered with her health, she was finally getting to live her life without endless hospital trips. How cruel life was to finally grant her the wish of her bookshop and then to dangle an attractive man in front of her when their relationship was doomed from the beginning. Prue decided to read on to the next entry, the day when her father came to the bookshop.

2nd June 1994 -

Dear diary,

I have had the best day ever! Love at first sight definitely does exist.

Robert Darwin is perfect in every single way. He made me laugh all day and I couldn't stop smiling just being in his presence. He's agreed to do the work on the bookshop and even made a little joke about us getting to spend so much time together. I showed him my sketches for the shop and he was as enthralled as I am. He can see my vision and that alone tells me what an amazing person he is.

And then diary, can you guess what happened next?

He asked me out on a date!

Of course I said yes. Mother is furious. Robert is one of the villagers now and apparently I shouldn't be 'mixing' with them. I told her I didn't care. The class system in Ivy Hatch is ridiculous. I'm just a normal girl (well as normal as you can get with a heart defect and a degree in art). If I want to go on a date with the hottest man in the village then I will.

We're going out for dinner on Friday night. I have to go shopping to find something new to wear!

Wish me luck diary!

◆ ◆ ◆

With a sense of sadness Prue put the diary down. Her mother had been so excited for her date, knowing how their story ended made Prue want to bury her head under the duvet and never come back out. How dare the villagers steal this happiness away from her mother! On a lighter note Prue had chuckled as her mother's thoughts immediately went to shopping and buying something new for her date. One thing Prue hadn't inherited from her mother was her love for vintage fashion. With a heavy sigh Prue stood up and stretched, she didn't know how to feel after reading those two diary entries. Sadness resounded throughout her and yet there was a happiness deep down. The chance to get an insight into her mother's thoughts was beyond anything Prue had ever expected to happen. She felt as though she was getting to know her mother.

Now all Prue had to do was decide whether or not she wanted to trace her father. As she got changed and climbed into bed she realised that there was no reason not to. Why shouldn't she meet her father? Surely he at least deserved to know she existed. Prue knew she might meet him and they might decide they didn't want a relationship but she had to know. She had to meet him. After all, she had gone twenty-four years without a father so what difference would it make if he rejected her? As her eyes drooped with sleep she tried to string together coherent thoughts to form a plan on how to track him down. It was too late though, she couldn't resist sleep any longer, it had been a very long day.

CHAPTER TWELVE

The following morning Prue woke feeling much calmer. It was somewhat of a relief to no longer have anger churning inside of her, today she could breathe and think coherently about what she had discovered last night. Prue grabbed her pale pink silk dressing gown and wrapped it around herself as she slipped her feet into her sheepskin slippers. It was bright sunshine outside but there was still a chilly breeze, despite it almost being May. With a coffee in hand she made her way outside and onto the lawn where a table and chairs sat. As the sun shone down Prue took a seat and looked around at the garden, the same grass that she had run on as a child. This was her home, it had been her family's home for generations, no amount of prejudice would make her leave.

Prue was grateful for her grandmother, for bringing her up to be a strong and independent woman, who knew her own mind. Nobody would sway Prue, once she had made a decision she would do everything within her power to see it through. This would be no different. The villagers would be hard to win over but she hoped that with a little negotiation they could live in harmony together. It was time that the younger generation adapted to the modern world and forgot about the divide between the Clemontes and the residents of Ivy Hatch.

As Prue sat watching the birds in the trees she began to form a plan in her head. She now knew that she wanted to track down her father, if that was at all possible. She hoped that Elliot might be able to help her. The second element of her plan involved charming the villagers. Despite their behaviour Prue knew she had to let that anger go or else she would never be happy here. If she harboured any bitterness towards the residents it would only eat away at her until she was unhappy and isolated. She planned on holding a meeting with everyone and discussing the changes she would be making to their contracts. Prue only hoped that would be enough to secure her acceptance in the village.

Draining the dregs of her coffee cup Prue stood up and stretched, it was time she put her plan into action. With a spring in her step she changed into a silk blush pink pleated midi skirt and a cream cashmere jumper. Prue was too impatient to do anything to her hair and so she styled it into a low bun. With a quick glance at her watch Prue grabbed the keys to the Bentley and made her way to Mr Adley's office. If she were being sensible she would have picked the Mini up from Elliot's but she wanted to save that trip for later. Prue was hoping to spend some time with Elliot and so she was planning on waiting until this evening to pick her car up. For now she had some important things to discuss with her solicitor.

The solicitor's office was silent as Prue walked in, the receptionist immediately jumped up and came running over to her.

'Miss Clemonte, I wasn't aware you had an appointment for today?' The woman was visibly flustered.

'It's okay, I don't have an appointment. Sorry I know Mr Adley is really busy but I was wondering whether he could see me quickly? I'm happy to come back in a while.'

'Of course, take a seat and I'll let Mr Adley know you're here. Can I get you anything, tea or coffee?' Despite having grown up in the manor it still irked Prue when people treated her differently. She wasn't special, she was just lucky enough to be born into a wealthy family. Well in her case perhaps she was unlucky to be born into a wealthy family.

An hour later Prue was walking back out of Mr Adley's office feeling somewhat more positive. They had agreed an overhaul on all contracts. The villagers would now be charged the market rent, no more or less, and before switching contracts they would have the option to terminate the agreement. If Prue was completely honest she hoped that a number of families would terminate their contract. She would do her best to be a gracious landlady but it was tough knowing that they had ruined her mother's happiness and prevented her from knowing her father. It was the right thing to do though, Mr Adley agreed that the changes should be made and he promised to start drawing up the new documents as soon as she left. They had agreed that in two weeks time she would arrange a meeting with the villagers to discuss the new contracts.

Now that her visit to Mr Adley was over with Prue could relax a little. She had put things in motion and there was no going back now. Either they accepted the changes or she would have to consider selling the properties. Prue knew that in the grand scheme of things she was a good landlady, the villagers paid their rent and the land and property was theirs to do what they wanted with. Who knew what rules other landlords would impose, surely they wouldn't want to take that risk? Doubt was beginning to form in Prue's mind.

No, Prue was their best option, they just had to realise that. Prue was doing this for her family's memory and for the village. Not for the villagers. With her first task of the day ticked off Prue climbed back into her car and began the journey home. Her next task was to stop at the farm shop on her way to buy some ingredients for dinner. The farm shop was one of the few places in the area that Prue didn't own and yet they were much nicer to her than all of her tenants put together. After a quick stop Prue picked up everything she needed to whip up a quick curry. She was going to surprise Elliot and bring dinner with her this afternoon. Thanks to him she could now take steps to resolve her problems. There was also the small matter that she wanted to spend some more time in his company.

The afternoon was spent in the kitchen at the manor with the windows open and music playing. Prue knew there would be plenty of time to worry about the villagers and finding her father but for now she needed some time out. Cooking was her relaxant, it always had been. During her time at university Prue supplied her entire halls with cake during exam periods. There was something just so relaxing about throwing various ingredients into a pan and creating something so delicious and rewarding.

Prue had text Elliot earlier telling him she would be over later and not to have dinner before she arrived. She had been a little ambitious sending that text thinking that she could wait until the evening to visit. Knowing that Elliot was working from home made it even harder to delay going round. There was something about his company that she really loved and his good looks were rather nice too. Prue sighed and put down the book she was holding, she had spent the last hour reading the same paragraph over and over. It was no good, she may as well go over to Elliot's now. With dinner in hand Prue slipped on some white pumps and walked down to Elliot's cottage.

He must have been looking out for her because as soon as she stepped foot on the cobbled pathway the front door swung open. Elliot stood there with a huge grin on his face. He was looking a little disheveled from working at home but even in his jogging bottoms and black t-shirt he still looked rather handsome. Prue almost ran down the little pathway and into the cottage. For a moment she wondered whether she enjoyed Elliot's company so much because he was the only person being nice to her. However, all those thoughts ebbed away as he leant forward to place a kiss on her cheek and her entire body felt as though an electric current had coursed through it.

Elliot took the dish from Prue and and put it in the kitchen for later, he then poured them both a drink and pointed Prue in the direction of the living room. It was a homely space with floor to ceiling bookshelves, almost bowing under the weight of hundreds of books. The flooring was the cottage's original stone but there were rugs covering most of it. At the back of the room was a big beige sofa which Prue sunk straight into. It was the kind of living room that you could curl up in, light a fire and while away the hours.

As the afternoon sun poured in and drenched them both in a golden glow Prue told Elliot all about her plans to renew the villager's contracts and make them fairer.

'You're doing more than they deserve.' Elliot observed, his eyes boring into hers.

'I know but I have no other option. I want to live here and be happy.' Prue felt the tears form in her eyes. All day she had kept busy trying to distract herself from the turmoil of emotions within her. Not five minutes with Elliot and she was crying again. He leant forward and enveloped her in a hug. Prue let herself relax into his embrace and took a few deep breaths to stop herself from crying.

'Thank you for being so kind.' She whispered as she pulled back slightly to look Elliot in the eye. As their eyes met she wasn't quite sure who moved first but suddenly his lips were against hers and they were kissing.

All too soon Elliot pulled back, a look of anguish on his face.

'I'm so sorry Prue, I shouldn't have done that. I've taken advantage of you.' He ran his fingers through his hair in a nervous gesture as Prue tried to speak around her tingling lips.

'Elliot, you didn't take advantage, I promise. I really like you.' Prue cringed as she heard her own words, she sounded like a fourteen year old confessing to fancying their crush.

'I really like you Prue.' He beamed back at her and reached out to hold her hand.

The evening was spent in a blissful bubble with just her and Elliot. They ate, drank and talked about everything and nothing. As much as Prue wanted to stay she knew she had to go home and so eventually she tore herself away from him but not before she got one final kiss.

CHAPTER THIRTEEN

It was Saturday morning and Prue woke up with a start. A couple of days had passed since she had last seen Elliot but he had been busy with work and so she had kept herself to herself. That didn't mean that they hadn't spoken though. For the past couple of nights they had both fallen asleep whilst on the phone to each other. Prue still felt a little thrill run through her every time she thought of him, she felt like a teenager again. She was finally getting to see Elliot again today. It wasn't exactly a date, they were going to try and find out some more information about her father.

Prue would be lying if she said she hadn't spent more time than usual on her hair and makeup. At 11am she emerged from her en-suite, finally happy with her appearance. It was about time too as there was a knock at the door. With one last glance in the mirror at her outfit Prue ran to the door. After much dithering she had finally settled on a plain grey tea dress and a chunky knit mustard coloured cardigan. Her hair had been curled to perfection and her makeup was flawless, yet natural. As Prue opened the door to Elliot she was surprised to see him looking so dapper, he had clearly taken note of her love for vintage fashion. He stood there in a tweed suit, a white shirt and a matching flat cap. It was so not his style and yet it suited him.

'You look very nice.' Prue commented, allowing him to step into the hallway.

'I'm sweltering already, might have to ditch the suit jacket.' He pulled off the jacket as he followed Prue into the kitchen where she had left her handbag.

'It suits you.' Prue smiled and reached up on her tiptoes to plant a kiss on his lips. The butterflies in her stomach started swarming as he wrapped his arms around her waist and pulled her in for a proper kiss.

As they made their way out to the front Prue slipped her hand into Elliot's and gave it a quick squeeze. It was a bittersweet day. Her first day spent with Elliot and yet here they were going in search of her father. Elliot had done some research and the last place they could trace her father to was a village on the coast about an hour's drive away. They had decided to make the most of the day and treat it as an almost-date. Prue could feel the excitement fizzing inside of her, a first date with Elliot and potentially finding her father, what a day.

'Can we take the Bentley?' Elliot turned to her with big round eyes, trying to use his good looks and charm to persuade her.

'I'm not sure, it's a long way. Can we not take your car?' As much as Prue loved her vintage cars she didn't know how reliable they would be on a longer journey.

Reluctantly, Elliot climbed into the driver's seat of his little Clio and they set off for the coast. Prue was aware that she should probably have been feeling nervous at the prospect of hunting down her father. However, after experiencing such a roller coaster of emotions over the past couple of weeks all she felt now was excitement. Her mind was made up, she had a plan in place and so now she could enjoy every second of it.

The drive down was fun. It was yet another lovely but chilly day, May was finally here and the sun had come out to celebrate. They listened to the radio and exchanged memories of seaside holidays as children. Prue's experiences were very different from Elliot's. As a child her boarding school would take her year group down to the seaside for a little holiday. She remembered it being so much fun being surrounded by her friends. In contrast, Elliot's family would go to the seaside on a day trip as their one treat of the summer holidays. Despite their differences it was clear that they both had the same appreciation for those short breaks from real life.

As they arrived at the little beachside town Elliot parked in the public car park and went to pay. Prue stepped out of the car and looked at her surroundings. The place looked just the same as it had ten years ago, in fact she suspected it hadn't changed since the 50s. The faded deckchairs were still lined up on the promenade with a handful of people sat in them. In the distance stood the pier which housed a rickety-looking helter-skelter with peeling paint and a rather bumpy landing. Prue remembered riding that helter-skelter as a child, the thrill of spinning down the side as you looked out to sea. It wasn't a memory that she wanted to relive though, especially given that she would most likely end up stuck halfway down, wedged between the wooden sides.

'You ready?' Elliot called, making Prue jump. She swivelled round to look at him and shot him a quick smile. This was it, they were going in search of her father. Elliot had the address folded up in his back pocket, he had apparently looked it up last night so that he knew how to get there from the car park. Prue couldn't thank him enough for his support, she didn't know how she would have got herself through this without him by her side.

Holding hands they walked in silence up a shaded hill with houses either side. Despite the dilapidated look the houses still had a quaint English seaside feel about them. As they reached the top of the hill and the pavement began to flatten out they took one of the roads to the left. The view from up here was amazing and the houses were situated so that their windows overlooked the dazzling sea below.

'It's that house there.' With a jolt Prue eye's turned to where Elliot was pointing. There was a 1920s style house with big bay windows looking out towards the sea. The garden out front was neatly kept, complete with a little flower bed around the edge. First impressions were good. It suddenly hit Prue that her father could be on the other side of that door. He could even have been hiding behind the net curtains looking towards the odd couple staring up at his house. A sudden wave of nerves crashed over Prue, during all this time she had been so excited at the idea of meeting her father she hadn't thought about what he might think. He probably didn't even know she existed. What if he didn't like her?

'Are you ready?' Elliot asked, giving her hand a reassuring squeeze. Unable to speak Prue just nodded and allowed Elliot to lead her up to the front door. There was a pause, as he waited for her to lean forward and knock but when she didn't move he leant forward and tapped on the door himself. The noise echoed throughout Prue's head. By now her hands were trembling and she had tears in her eyes. The sudden realisation that her father might reject her had hit her hard. She had enough to contend with at home, trying to win over an entire village, the last thing she needed was to have to persuade her father to love her. Prue wanted to run away, as far as she possibly could, however Elliot's hand in hers kept her anchored to the spot. She had to be brave and do this or else she would always wonder what might have been.

After a tense few seconds the door swung open and a middle aged woman stood there staring back at them. Prue's head was pounding as she took in the woman stood in front of her. Was this her father's wife? Perhaps he had other children. She could have half siblings just on the other side of this door. Her brain was too scrambled to speak but thankfully she had Elliot by her side who seemed to sense that she was in no fit state to start a conversation.

'Sorry to disturb you. I'm wondering if you can help us, we're looking for a Robert Darwin?' Elliot was as charming as ever.

'I'm sorry but we bought the property from Robert almost five years ago.' Prue felt disappointment wash over her, she had been so close to meeting her father and yet it had been so cruelly pulled away from her. Knowing that he had been there but she was five years too late crushed her.

'Would you happen to have a forwarding address?' Prue's ears perked up again, she was so thankful to have Elliot with her as he was able to think and speak coherently.

'I'm afraid not. Sorry I can't help you.' The woman was polite but curt, it was clear that she didn't wish to stand on the doorstop talking any longer. Elliot said their thanks and half dragged Prue back down the pathway. She didn't quite know how to process what had just happened, all she knew was that she felt exhausted from the flood of emotions.

'Come on, let's find somewhere to sit down and have a coffee.' Elliot took her hand again and led her back towards the seafront. Prue followed blindly, hardly taking in her surroundings.

Eventually they came across a little cafe by the promenade which sold fish and chips. It was almost empty and so they chose a table by the window and Elliot ordered them both a coffee.

'How are you? Sorry that's a silly question isn't it.' For the first time today even Elliot didn't know what to say.

'Thank you for doing this Elliot.' Prue smiled and reached across the table to hold his hand.

'I'm sorry we didn't find your father today, Prue. I promise you that we'll keep trying.'

Elliot's resilience gave Prue a little boost, he was right they could keep trying. One failed attempt didn't mark the end, it was just the beginning of the search.

CHAPTER FOURTEEN

To say Prue was disappointed, after their failed attempt to find her father would be an understatement. However, it had fuelled her motivation to find him. They had traced him to one of his previous addresses and so it was only a matter of time before they eventually discovered his current location. Elliot had been searching all week, asking contacts and looking into local records but nobody seemed to know anything about Robert Darwin. Meanwhile, Prue had busied herself setting up a meeting with the villagers on Saturday evening. After some persuasion she had arranged for everyone to meet at the cafe. It was now Friday evening and she was a ball of nerves but not just because of Saturday's meeting. After their disastrous first date Elliot had asked to take Prue out for dinner this evening. Like a teenager with a crush she had giggled and accepted and so here she was standing in front of the mirror scrutinising her outfit.

Prue was the first to admit that her fashion sense was a little unusual, for this era anyway. Tonight she had opted for a pair of bright red swing trousers and a white silk blouse. Her hair was in its trademark curls and she had even taken the time to match her lips to the colour of her trousers. Prue hoped that it was good enough for wherever they were going. The nerves only worsened as Prue heard Elliot's car coming up the drive. It was silly, she'd seen him a few nights during the week. The fact that tonight was labelled as a date had added a layer of stress and expectations. Prue always worried that people judged her on appearance, however when they got to know her she was far from a 1940's housewife. She was opinionated and motivated and nobody would stand in her way when she set her mind to something. Prue only hoped that Elliot was being genuine with her and not just looking to wind his father up by dating public enemy number one.

Elliot had promised to take her for dinner somewhere that nobody would recognise her and for that she was grateful. The last thing she wanted was to have people whispering about her and shooting her hateful glances as she tried to relax on their date. Elliot beeped his car horn letting her know that he was there. Prue took a deep breath to steady her nerves and made her way outside to greet him. Elliot was standing next to his car dressed in black skinny jeans and a white shirt. Prue felt herself swoon slightly as she took in his appearance.

'You look amazing.' Elliot smiled as he gave her a quick kiss before opening the car door for her.

'You look amazing too.' Prue shot him a quick smile as she climbed into the passenger side of his car.

A few minutes later they were driving along the road that led out of the village. Prue felt herself relax as they left the hostile environment behind them and headed towards their date. Now that she was with Elliot and they were outside the village her nerves had turned into excitement at the prospect of an evening in his company. Rather than asking lots of questions about where they were going Prue tried to relax and just enjoy the journey with Elliot by her side.

All too soon they were turning into a little side-road with an inn to the left. It was beautiful, with ivy growing all around the imposing Georgian building. There were lit torches on either side of the front door and above it in fancy lettering was the name 'The Bullfinch'. It looked beautiful and very out of place in the middle of nowhere.

'It's a little over the top and it's a tourist hotspot but I knew we'd be safe from any of the villagers.' Elliot explained as he saw the awe on Prue's face.

'It's beautiful. I'm quite excited now.'

With a smile on both their faces they walked hand in hand into the pub and were seated at one of the tables towards the back of the restaurant. The Bullfinch had an air of discreetness about it. The lights were dimmed and the tables were set far apart, giving everyone their own privacy. It may not have been what Prue was used to but it was perfect for their first dinner date. The waiter came to take their drink orders and before they had even had the chance to look at the menu a bottle of red wine was presented to them.

'I want to come here for dinner every night.' Prue sighed, feeling content with a glass of wine in hand and a risotto on its way. She wanted to remember every second of this evening sitting here with such an amazing person staring back at her. Elliot's eyes were soft as he asked her questions about her childhood and leaned forward in interest, listening to her replies.

'So what about you Elliot Harrington? So far I know that you're a rebellious character who enjoys winding up his father. What were you like at university?'

'I'm afraid I might be a bit of a disappointment to you. I wasn't very rebellious, unless you consider drinking on a Tuesday evening rebellious?'

'I'm afraid not. Where did you go to university?' Prue wanted to know everything she could about the bewildering man sat opposite her.

'I went to Sussex.' His answer was short as the food was placed down in front of them by an over eager waiter who slopped Elliot's gravy all over the table. Prue sat in silence watching as the waiter apologised over and over whilst mopping up the mess. They had gone to the same university. Fate was something that Prue believed deeply in, it was a mindset that she had been forced to adopt from a young age after losing her mother. Everything happens for a reason. If their paths had almost crossed before, was that fate? Had fate been trying to pull them together for years?

'We were at the same university.' Prue commented once the waiter had cleared up the mess and walked away.

'We would have been there around the same time too, unless you took a year out?'

'No, I went straight to university. It's crazy to think that we've been living so close to each other for our entire lives and we've only just met properly.'

The night was a blur of good food and brilliant conversation. Prue felt herself becoming even more enthralled by Elliot's charm and good nature. They may have come from different backgrounds but they were united in being outcasts. Prue was convinced that they were meant to be together, they had been living their lives in parallel just waiting for their paths to cross.

By the end of the night Prue's face hurt from laughing so much, she was sure she had never had so much fun on a date before. Like a gentleman Elliot drove her home and left her on the doorstep with a kiss. He had promised to come over the following afternoon and help her prepare for her impending meeting with the villagers. Prue was giddy with excitement and lust as she let herself into the manor and took herself straight to bed.

Once in bed she found herself wondering what her mother and father's first date had been like. The diary was still on her window seat, where she had left it, and so she climbed out of bed and sat down next to it. The moonlight was flooding in from the gap in the curtains, the light reflecting off of the dragonfly on the cover of the diary. Prue couldn't wait any longer, she wanted to know how their first date had gone.

◆ ◆ ◆

3rd June 1994

I suppose I should have dated this entry 4th June 1994 since it's now 2am but the evening started on the 3rd.

Oh diary, I've had the best night of my life. Robert picked me up at 6pm, as promised. The look on mother's face was hilarious as he pulled up outside the manor in his beaten up Ford. She gave me a look and without a word turned and shut herself in the library. I know that despite her coldness she'll still want to hear about my night over breakfast tomorrow.

I bought a new dress for the date, a little black dress. Feeling very grown up I made my way outside to see Robert stood there in a suit! He looked amazing.

We drove a little way out of the village and he took me to a little pub. It was small and quaint but perfect. We ate dinner in the candle light and I didn't stop smiling all night.

Diary, I am certain that there's nothing about Robert that I could ever dislike. After tonight, I'm convinced he's my soulmate.

Once we had finished dinner we bought a bottle of wine and took it back to the bookshop. The shop may be a shell at the moment but we still had a lovely time. We spread a blanket out on the floor, lit some candles and just sat there talking for hours and hours on end.

Finally, he dropped me off at the bottom of the drive and gave me a kiss goodnight.

I'm seeing him again tomorrow.

Goodnight diary.

Prue's emotions were mixed as she put the diary back down. She felt a happiness within her at the thought of how much her parents had enjoyed their first date. It sounded like perfection. However, a small part of Prue's brain couldn't help but realise how similar their dates had been. Was history about to repeat itself in Ivy Hatch? With a heavy feeling in her heart Prue made her way back to bed and laid there in the darkness trying to empty her mind. History couldn't repeat itself, Prue wouldn't let it.

CHAPTER FIFTEEN

The ball of nerves in the pit of Prue's stomach returned with a vengeance the following morning. Well, that and a disgusting red wine hangover. Elliot had been driving last night and so she had polished off the entire bottle, bar one glass, on her own. Prue was also still going over her mother's diary entry that she had read last night, it had left her with an odd feeling. All-in-all she was feeling rather fragile on the day that she needed to be at her best. Prue wrapped her dressing gown around herself, slid her feet into her slippers and made her way downstairs to make a coffee. As she was half way down the stairs she stopped as she caught sight of the mess in the hallway. Her heart rate picked up and she felt her stomach churning. The pane of glass next to the front door was shattered and on the floor lay a brick with what looked like a note wrapped around it. With tears in her eyes Prue sat down on the step and pulled her phone out, she couldn't cope with this on her own. With her friends in Brighton so far away there was only one person Prue could call. With trembling hands she scrolled through her phonebook for Elliot's number.

'Elliot Harrington speaking.' Despite everything Prue still felt a thrill go through her at the sound of Elliot's sleepy voice.

'Elliot, it's Prue. Sorry have I woken you?' As hard as she tried, Prue couldn't keep the tremble from her voice.

'Prue, what's wrong?' Elliot sounded wide awake now. Prue took a deep breath, she hated having to rely on someone else but what else could she do? She was scared.

'I was wondering if you could come up to the manor. Now.' Prue was too frightened to prioritise her independence right now. Who knew who had thrown that brick, they could still be lurking outside. With a sudden chill Prue realised she hadn't even been able to check the backdoor. What if there was someone in the house with her?

'Prue, what's going on?' Elliot asked, there was the sound of movement and a jingle of keys.

'Someone's thrown a brick through the window.' Saying it out loud made it feel real. Up until now Prue had felt like she was in a dream, staring down at someone else's problem. It was her problem though and only she could rectify it. Elliot stayed on the phone to Prue until he pulled up outside and she was forced to move from the stairs to unlock the door. As soon as the door was unlocked he pulled Prue into his arms and slowly the tears began to fall, landing onto what looked to be Elliot's pyjama top. Eventually Prue pulled back and Elliot took her hand in his, squeezing it gently.

'Did you see anyone?' He asked, as they both looked around at the mess and the shattered glass littering almost every surface.

'No. I think there might be a note attached to the brick.' Prue pointed towards the weapon, lying surreptitiously in the middle of the hallway. She went to walk over to it but Elliot pulled her back.

'You mustn't touch anything until after the police have been.'

Prue was taken back by the statement. She hadn't even thought of contacting the police, it would make sense but did she really want to continue to anger whoever had done this? Prue didn't need to do much soul searching to know the answer to that question. She didn't want to anger anyone. There was a part of her that was angry and frightened but she didn't want to risk things escalating even further. This had been a wake-up call, she really was hated in the village and this was the proof.

'I don't think I want to call the police.'

Elliot looked at her in shock. She knew he must be thinking she was crazy, there was a part of her that was thinking the same. She had to weigh everything up though and she couldn't risk anything else happening to the manor. Or the bookshop. With a sudden jolt Prue realised that the shop could have been targeted too. What if they had got into the shop and stripped it of all the books? All those handwritten notes that her mother had left there. That shop was a treasure trove of memories for Prue and she couldn't bear the thought of anything happening to them.

'I'm not going to push you into calling the police Prue but think about it. Whoever has done this to you is trying to scare you, going to the police is a natural reaction.'

Prue knew that Elliot was making a valid argument but still, she didn't want to make things worse. She was stuck and the villagers knew that. Retaliate and she wound wind them up even more. She would be forced to play the long game. Prue would attend the meeting that afternoon and be as charming and lovely to the villagers as she possibly could. This was her home too and she was going to show them that. If they didn't like it then they could leave. With her mind made up Prue made her way over towards the brick, careful not to tread on any of the broken glass. She picked up the weapon with trembling hands and undid the elastic band which was holding the note to it.

Elliot made his way over towards her as she unwrapped the note. It was brief and to the point, only stating 'You're not welcome here.'

'I already knew that, they didn't need to throw a brick through my window.' Prue tried to lighten the mood but Elliot's face was ashen.

'What's wrong?' She asked, watching as a mixture of unknown

emotions flickered across his face.

'Prue I'm so sorry. I recognise that handwriting, it's my father's.'

They were both silent as it sank in. Nothing was ever smooth in life but having your boyfriend's dad try to run you out of town was a whole new experience for Prue.

'Is your dad usually this overprotective of you?' Prue asked, breaking the awkward silence that hung in the room.

'Prue this is all my fault. My father must have found out that we've been dating.' The torment on Elliot's face almost broke Prue's heart in two. He looked so guilty, as if he was solely responsible for his father's vile actions.

'Elliot, please listen to me. What your father does is up to him, please don't for one second feel guilty about his actions. I'm a grown adult and I'm choosing to stay in this village, despite the resistance from the villagers. I will therefore also choose who I go on dates with.' Prue's fiery nature was beginning to fight its way to the surface. She wasn't going to go to the police but she would show the village that she wasn't scared. This village was hers, after all she owned most of it. Nobody would scare her away, nor would they tell her who she could or couldn't date.

The day passed quickly as Elliot stayed with Prue and helped her tidy up. Thankfully there was no more damage either to the manor or to the gardens. Prue was fearful of spending the night there on her own again but she was pushing that to the back of her mind, for now she had to concentrate on the meeting that she had that afternoon. Time was getting on and Prue was ready. She had decided that she would go and check on the bookshop before the meeting and so both her and Elliot left at the same time. He went home to get ready whilst she drove herself into the village.

With fear in her heart Prue made her way along the cobbled path to the door of the bookshop. She paused for a moment, building up the courage to go in. She had only just discovered the shop and its connection to her mother. There were so many more memories encased within these walls and Prue was only just starting to discover them. Please don't let anyone have been inside the shop, Prue silently begged as she turned the key in the door.

Thankfully the shop was intact and everything was how Prue had left it on Friday afternoon. The place was spotless as the spine of each book reflected the sun. There was nothing left to do inside the shop, it was ready to open. However, Prue was reluctant to allow her enemies into such a private space. The connection she felt to her mother inside that little shop was something she wanted to cherish forever and so it would be a difficult decision to open the place up.

Prue's phone buzzed with a message from Elliot telling her that he had just arrived at the cafe and everyone was there waiting for her, even his father. With one final look around the shop Prue soaked up the essence of her mother's sprit. It was time she fought for herself, for her family and for a better future for the village.

CHAPTER SIXTEEN

As Prue walked into the cafe every pair of eyes fell on her. The atmosphere was tangible and it was clear that everyone, besides Elliot, loathed being in her company. This was business though, not pleasure. Whether they liked it or not Prue was their landlady and they had to hear what she was about to say. For once Prue felt as though she had the upper hand and she took a moment to relish in that feeling. Slowly she walked up to the table of refreshments and poured herself a coffee, opting to treat herself by pouring cream in rather than milk. She knew that she was still being watched by everyone and so she slowed her actions down even more. After everything they had put her through she would make them suffer by waiting that bit longer to hear what she had to say.

After taking the first sip of her coffee Prue took a deep breath and turned around to face the crowded room. Everyone was scowling at her. Prue wanted to run and hide away at the manor but she knew that wouldn't help the situation. She had to be nice. In fact she had to be really nice. Thank god for those drama classes she had taken at school. With a huge smile on her face Prue moved towards the front of the room, taking each step slowly. By now she had the whole room hanging on her every move and she was enjoying it. The villagers knew that whatever she had to say would either make or break them and Prue was enjoying every second of them not knowing. With a final glance over at Elliot, who shot her a reassuring smile, Prue stood in front of the room of people and turned to address them.

'Thank you for all agreeing to meet me here today. As I'm sure you already know, refreshments are complimentary so please help yourself.'

Prue was cut off by some angry grunts towards the back of the room.

'Can I help you?' She called with a sickly grin on her face. No matter how angry they made her she would not let it show. Prue would be the best landlady that they could ever wish for.

'Complimentary? Our rent is paying for this spread!' The anger in the man's voice resounded throughout the small space. If the villagers hadn't run her father out of town and ruined her mother's chances at happiness then Prue might have found herself feeling sorry for them.

'That's what we're here to discuss.' Everyone quietened down and many people took their seats as they all waited to hear what Prue had to say.

Feeling brave Prue explained to the room her plans to give each village member a new contract, a fairer contract. They could either sign it and work in harmony with her or they were free to walk away. As she spoke Prue could feel the atmosphere in the room change, the hostility was ebbing away and she could see private conversations breaking out amongst the crowds. Prue's face may have looked steely but her insides were churning, if this didn't work she wasn't sure how she would resolve the community's anger so that they could live in harmony. Right now, this was her only option and it had to work.

There was a moment of silence as Prue finished her speech and the crowd digested what she had to say. Prue used that time to steady her breathing and took a sip of her coffee, wishing it was something much stronger.

'Does anyone have any questions?' Prue asked, she couldn't bear the silence for much longer, she just wanted to know how her plans had been received.

‘Will we have to pay to exit the contract?’ Prue glanced towards the man, he was sat in the corner with his hat pulled down to cover most of his face. It took Prue a minute to recall who he was but eventually she recognised him as the village mechanic. Prue was going to be busy replacing those who left to ensure there was still a basic infrastructure for those who chose to stay in the village.

‘No, there will be no fee but I’d appreciate it if you could give me a month’s notice. For those of you that choose to stay I will do my best to ensure every business remains operating with a new proprietor. I understand that every business is needed and I want to prevent as much disruption as I can.’ There were lots of nods from amongst the crowd, Prue felt as though she had finally made some progress with the villagers.

‘Can the contracts include a clause that we can purchase the property from you?’ This question was from the lady who owned the cafe.

‘That’s not something I had considered but if that’s something everyone would like then I can talk to my solicitor about including the clause?’ Prue was taken back, she hadn’t expected them to ask if they could buy the property. It made sense though, it would allow the village to thrive and grow, it would also reduce Prue’s responsibility.

‘What do you want in exchange for this?’ Prue’s head snapped up as she recognised the voice and the venomous tone. It was Elliot’s father, stood at the back of the room surrounded by a group of fellow farmers.

‘All I want is a quiet life. I would also appreciate it if people would stop throwing bricks through my window.’ Prue tried to keep her tone light so nobody suspected that the dig was aimed at Arnold Harrington. He knew she was addressing him and his eyes narrowed as he realised she wasn’t going to stand down and accept defeat. Prue was here to fight for herself.

There were no more questions and so Prue decided to leave rather than staying to mingle with the crowd. It had gone better than she had expected and so she had to quit while she was ahead. She also didn't want to come into contact with Elliot's father, there was still anger bubbling away under her happy facade and the last thing she needed was to let her true feelings show. With a quick smile at Elliot, Prue slipped out of the cafe as everyone was talking and helping themselves to the refreshments. The atmosphere had changed completely and almost everyone seemed content with what Prue had said. Prue only hoped that she had done enough. Only time would tell.

Prue breathed a sigh of relief as the cool air hit her and she left behind the noise of the crowd. It was over and now all she had to do was wait and see how the village would adjust to the new way of life. The new contracts would be with them within the next week and then Prue would have to see who decided to sign and who decided to walk away. She was eager for the next few weeks to whiz by as she wanted to pour all of her focus into the bookshop. For now though, she would continue to keep visiting it and reading the little slips of paper that her mother had left within the cover of each book. A small but precious insight into her mother's mind. One day she would be able to give the shop the grand re-opening that it deserved but that day would have to wait.

CHAPTER SEVENTEEN

After the meeting Prue drove her car to Elliot's cottage and let herself in with the spare key he had given her. They had agreed that it would be safer for her to stay the night with him so they could see how the village would react. Prue hated the thought of the manor laying empty with nobody there to protect it but for now she had to look after herself. The last thing she needed was a confrontation with an angry mob just as she was making some progress. As Prue walked into Elliot's cottage the silence was comforting, having gone from such a busy room to solitude was bliss. Growing up an only child Prue had learnt to appreciate her own company from a young age.

Elliot had told her to make herself comfortable and so she took her bag of clothes upstairs and changed into a fresh set of pyjamas. They were a gorgeous emerald green silk set that her friend Katie had got her for Christmas last year. Putting them on made her think of her friend and Prue found herself yearning for the life she had left behind in Brighton. She had been free, no responsibilities and she could walk down the street without anyone glaring at her. Brighton had been a form of solace for her soul. A place to grow into herself without the judgment and expectations of an entire village on her. That safe haven would always hold a special place in her heart but it wasn't home. Home was here, in this village with the memories of her mother and her grandmother.

Resisting the urge to have a look around the cottage whilst she was on her own Prue decided to go and make a start on dinner. Elliot had warned her he might be a while as he wanted to stay and talk to his father. Prue didn't want to even consider how that conversation might be going and so she turned up the music on her phone and began to rifle through Elliot's fridge looking for items that she could use to throw together something that resembled dinner. A glass of wine and a few ABBA tunes later Prue was feeling much more positive.

'Honey, I'm home!' Elliot called as the front door swung open. It was good timing as the alarm on Prue's phone had just gone off to alert her that the pasta bake was cooked. The contents of Elliot's kitchen had been a sorry state and so Prue had made the best of what was there.

'You're just in time, dinner's ready.' Prue smiled and ran over to give him a quick peck on the lips. His arms wrapped around her waist and he pulled her in for a deeper kiss she squealed and pulled herself out of his grip.

'Stop it, dinner will get ruined.' Before he could grab her again she ran off towards the kitchen. There was a genuine smile on her face and she felt as though a huge weight had been lifted from her shoulders. If only for this evening she could completely relax in Elliot's company and enjoy herself.

'How did the chat with your dad go?' Prue asked as she put her fork down, dinner had been a success. Elliot's face changed as she mentioned his father, the carefree look vanished and his brow knitted with stress. Perhaps she shouldn't have asked that question. Prue tried to put it to the back of her mind, it wouldn't do either of them any good to dwell on it.

'I think it's best we forget about my father Prue. I've told him not to go near you or the manor again and I hope he'll listen to me.' Elliot's voice sounded detached and far away. Whatever had been said it obviously hadn't been a loving reunion between the two men.

'How do you think the meeting went?' Prue asked, trying to lead the conversation away from Elliot and his father.

'It went really well Prue, I'm so proud of you.' He leant across the table and took her hand in his. 'Once you left everyone stayed to talk about the new contracts and the majority seemed to be happy. I think you might find a few people choose to leave but perhaps that's for the best. We could do with some new faces around here.'

Prue felt her heart soar as she heard Elliot's feedback. Perhaps things were about to change and she would find herself able to walk down the street without worrying someone might throw rotten eggs at her. She hoped so, she wasn't exactly asking for much.

That evening Prue felt like she was in a little bubble with Elliot by her side. She was relaxed and happy, it felt like nothing would ever be able to wipe that smile off of her face. As they curled up on the sofa together, with a well deserved glass of wine, Prue kept sneaking glances at Elliot. How had she been so lucky to come across this man when she hadn't even been looking for love? A jolt went through Prue as she realised the word love had just flitted across her brain. Did she really love him? Prue took a large sip of wine to busy herself whilst she tried to get her thoughts under control. Elliot turned to look at her and shot her a heart stopping smile. In that moment she knew it was true, she did love him.

CHAPTER EIGHTEEN

Waking up the following morning in Elliot's arms only sent Prue's mood flying even higher. She needed some help at the bookshop today, as she couldn't lift the big round table on her own. Elliot had offered to help her and so they were going to spend the day giving the shop a final once over. After the positive response from the village last night Prue had decided to open the bookshop earlier than planned. Next Saturday would be the opening day and she was already buzzing with excitement at the prospect of her little bookshop being filled with people looking for their next read.

'Good morning sleeping beauty.' Elliot whispered in her ear as he hugged her closer to him.

'Morning.' She smiled back at him. It would be nice to wake up like this every day.

After a slow morning and a delicious brunch, left on the doorstep by Elliot's mother, they got ready for the day. Prue was apprehensive, yet excited at the prospect of going into the village and to see how everyone reacted to her. Would anything have changed or would the hostility continue? She knew she would have to face it at some point and it was better to get it over with when she had Elliot by her side.

They set off towards the village, hand in hand. It was a lovely day out and so they had opted to walk in. As they made their way to the bookshop Prue noticed they received a number of looks. However, the looks had lost their hostile edge, instead they seemed to be curious. It was a nice change but Prue still didn't enjoy being scrutinised by everyone, she longed for the anonymity of the bigger cities.

'This place is amazing.' Elliot's reaction to the bookshop never failed to make Prue smile. He was as enthralled with the little shop as she was.

'I know. Whenever I'm in here I can imagine my mother standing behind the counter or sitting in that chair reading her favourite book. There's just something so magical about all the memories that this little place holds.'

'My mother loves reading but she has to hide it from my father. He views it as a waste of her time when she could be doing something like cooking dinner or washing his clothes.'

The more Prue heard about Elliot's family life the sadder she felt for him. How terrible to grow up in a house where you couldn't express yourself or indulge in a few minutes of something that made you happy.

'Elliot please tell your mother that she's always welcome here. She can stay and read for as long as she likes.'

Prue's idea for the little shop was to be a part of the community, to provide a safe and calm space for people to come and enjoy reading. She only hoped she could do her mother justice and convey her vision.

By the end of the day the little shop was looking perfect, all that was missing now were the customers. Prue looked around and felt her heart almost burst with pride, this was her mother's creation but now it was all hers and she had to make a success of it.

'Are you ready to go?' Elliot asked her as he came back from washing his paint brush. Prue had decided to hand paint '*The Vintage Bookshop of Memories*' on the front counter in the colour antique gold. A skill that Katie had taught her. It was a final touch and one that really pulled everything together.

'Can we stay at the manor tonight?' The plan had been for her to stay at Elliot's over the weekend but Prue knew she had to go home at some point. She would feel safer if Elliot stayed with her for a couple of nights. They agreed to go back to the manor, with a slight detour so that Elliot could pack a bag for himself.

As they drove up to the gate of the manor Prue felt a sickening feeling in her stomach, something wasn't right. It took her a few seconds to realise what was so out of place. Her entire body was trembling as she looked towards the front of the manor, the front door had been smashed in and there was nothing in its place. Prue could see straight into the hallway where everything had been vandalised. A chill ran down Prue's spine as she realised anyone could just walk in or out of the manor.

'Elliot?' Prue whispered, she wasn't sure whether or not he had noticed it yet.

'I'm calling the police this time Prue. We're not going in until they've been. Who knows what or who could be inside.'

Prue knew Elliot was right, it had gone too far this time and she needed to put her foot down. She sat in silence staring at her home as Elliot called the police and told them what had happened. It only took the police ten minutes to arrive, however every one of those minutes seemed to stretch on for an eternity. Prue was barely able to consider what the inside of the manor might look like. The hallway had been completely desecrated, who knew what they had done to the rest of the house. Precious memories gone or vandalised. Everything she had was here in this house and there was someone out there trying to take that from her. The worst thing was it was highly likely that the someone was Elliot's father.

The police arrived and there was a sudden buzz of action. In a somewhat dazed state Prue answered all of their questions and watched as they combed the house for any evidence. Other than a smashed door and the vandalism in the hallway all the police found were some graffiti on the walls.

'What does the graffiti say?' Prue almost didn't recognise her voice, she sounded detached and cold. She was putting all of her effort into keeping herself together, she couldn't afford to let her emotions free right now, not until the police had left.

'It says 'you're not welcome here'.' A chill ran down Prue's spine as the police officer turned to Elliot to ask him if he knew who might have done it. Elliot shook his head, his face completely blank and told the officer that he didn't know who may have done such a thing.

As the officer turned to her Prue had an internal battle with herself, she knew exactly who had done this but should she tell the police? The graffiti was word for word the same as the note wrapped around the brick.

'It was Arnold Harrington. He also threw a brick through my window.' Prue could see Elliot's eyes fall on her and the disappointment on his face. She didn't care. She had done everything in her power to appease the village and it seemed to be working. It was time that Arnold realised that he couldn't keep stirring up trouble with her. He had to take responsibility for his actions and be punished for them.

The police took Prue to one side so that she could give them a statement. She could feel Elliot's eyes on her the entire time but she couldn't turn to look at him. Prue understood that he was in a difficult situation but she refused to continue living her life in fear. What would his father do next?

Eventually the police left, after boarding up the doorway and telling her to call them if she needed anything. Prue watched the officers drive back down the driveway and a part of her almost wished they would come back. With them gone it was just her and Elliot and she knew they would have to talk about what had just happened. With some reluctance Prue walked around the back of the manor so that they could go in through the back door. It was a horrible feeling to know that someone had been inside your home spreading such hate. A part of her didn't want to even go inside but she knew she had to be strong, this was her home and it would continue to be her home. She would not let one single-minded farmer scare her out of her family home.

'Why did you tell them it was my father?' Elliot broke the silence between them once they were inside the house with the backdoor shut.

'I had to Elliot. He keeps coming to my house and vandalising things. He's trying to scare me into leaving my home. I've grown up here, why should I leave? It's as much my home as it is yours. It's not right, Elliot.'

There was a tense silence between them as Elliot processed what she had to say. She could tell that he was struggling with an internal battle, he knew she was right and yet it was still his father.
'Perhaps you should go home Elliot.' As much as Prue didn't want to be on her own here, she knew right now they needed their space.

'I can't leave you here on your own.' He replied, his face full of torment.

'You can. I'm going to call a friend and ask her to come and stay for a bit. Honestly, I'll be fine.' Prue was putting on a brave face, she couldn't let on how scared she really was because then Elliot wouldn't leave.

Eventually, Elliot accepted her reassurance and he left, with just a peck on her cheek. Once Prue was sure he was gone she let herself succumb to her emotions and ran up to her bedroom and cried. She felt completely lost in the world, torn in two. She was yearning for her life back in Brighton and yet she was loving being at home surrounded by her memories. This turmoil was only fuelling her want to find her father, it would be nice to have someone completely on her side and to help her fight her battles against the village.

Once her tears had stopped falling Prue took a deep breath and pulled out her phone, she had been meaning to invite Katie to come and stay and right now she could do with a friendly face.

'Hello?' Prue couldn't help but smile as she heard Katie's perky voice down the phone, she had really missed her friend.

'Katie, I've missed you!' Prue knew that Katie would immediately know something was wrong from the tone of her voice.

'Prue, what's wrong?' Twenty minutes later Prue had told Katie what had been happening and they had arranged for Katie to come and stay. She would get the train down tomorrow morning and Prue would pick her up just after lunchtime.

Once Prue had put the phone down she considered going downstairs and making herself some dinner. However, the thought of walking through the dark house on her own scared her and so she decided to just write the day off and go to bed early. She locked her bedroom door and moved the heavy scalloped green armchair in front of it, in an attempt to barricade herself in. It was ridiculous that she had to go to such lengths to feel even the slightest bit safe in her own home. Anger was bubbling away inside of Prue and she knew it would fuel her to keep going and to fight this battle. Hopefully tomorrow would be a better day.

CHAPTER NINETEEN

The following morning Prue woke to someone knocking on her boarded up door. She hoped it was Elliot coming to apologise for how sour things had turned last night. Prue couldn't allow herself to think who else it might be, if she did then she would be paralysed with fear. After wrapping her dressing gown around herself she tiptoed downstairs to see who it was. Thankfully, there was still one window intact by the side of the boarded up doorway and so she could peek out. As Prue caught a glimpse of who was on the other side of the door she felt her heart pound and her hands tremble. Staring straight back at her was Arnold Harrington. Prue didn't know what to do, she couldn't run anywhere, she was trapped.

'I just want to talk.' Arnold said, he must have seen the terrified look on Prue's face. His voice was gruff and he was holding his hands up in a gesture of surrender. There wasn't anything Prue could do other than appease him and so she called back telling him she would be a minute. A part of her was interested to see what he had to say for himself. She ran upstairs and quickly threw on some clothes before grabbing her phone and putting it safely in her pocket. She also knew that the gardener would be round soon and so she wouldn't be completely alone for long. Prue let herself out through the backdoor and made her way round to the front of the manor. She took a few deep breaths to steady her nerves, she couldn't show Arnold any sign of weakness. She had to be strong and confident.

Each and every nerve inside of Prue's body was on edge and was screaming at her to run as far away as possible from the man who had been harassing her. However, she knew he would take great pleasure in seeing how scared his actions had made her and so she pushed away those feelings and with every step she came closer to Arnold Harrington.

'What do you want?' She spat as she came to stand in front of him. Prue wanted this little chat over with as quick as possible.

'I wanted to speak to you, to offer you an ultimatum.' His voice was gruff and his eyes were narrow in obvious disdain at the woman stood in front of him.

'What kind of ultimatum? Prue questioned, she was beginning to worry where this was going. She wouldn't be driven out of her home or out of the village by anyone, not even this brute of a man.

'I've heard rumours that you're looking for your father, is it true?'

Prue felt the anger boil up inside of her, she took a deep breath and dug her nails into the palm of her hands to stop herself from doing anything stupid.

'I don't see how that's any of your business.' She replied, thankfully the iciness of her tone hid the anger that was simmering away beneath the surface.

'It's my business because you're dating my son.' The disgust on Arnold's face was clear, he hated the thought of his son mixing with one of the Clemontes. There was a small part of Prue that was enjoying this.

'Whether I'm looking for my father or not is none of your business. Now I suggest you leave my property before I call the police.' Prue crossed her arms across her chest and stood tall, she wouldn't let him intimidate her.

'I know where your father is. If you end whatever is going on between you and Elliot I'll give you his address.' Prue was left stunned as she watched Arnold walk back down her driveway. That hadn't been the ultimatum that she had been expecting.

Once Prue was safely back inside the manor with the door locked behind her she took a seat at the breakfast bar and placed her head in her hands. She didn't know what to do. As lovely as her relationship with Elliot was it seemed doomed. Were they going to end the same way her own parents had? Perhaps it was best if things ended now to minimise the heartbreak. If Prue ended things it was possible that she would be able to find her father and the abuse from Arnold would stop. As much as she was falling in love with Elliot she knew that their relationship wouldn't survive his father's wrath. From their first date something had unnerved Prue, the similarities between their relationship and her parents had been worrying. She knew that if she didn't act soon they would be as heartbroken and as unhappy as her own parents had been.

Although it broke her heart Prue knew what she had to do. Taking the coward's way out she pulled her phone out from her pocket and began to draft a text to Elliot. She knew it would hurt him, especially doing it by text but she had to make him realise she was serious. If she spoke to him face-to-face there was the risk that her emotions would overcome her and she wouldn't be able to do what she had to do. The text was short and to the point, perhaps a little cold hearted but Prue knew it had to be that way. She thanked him for all of his support and kindness and told him that she appreciated it but unfortunately they couldn't keep seeing each other. Their relationship was strictly professional if they ever bumped into each other at the solicitor's office.

Once she had hit send Prue hid her phone in one of the kitchen drawers and wiped a stray tear that was slowly sliding down her face. She had to be strong and so she took a deep breath and went upstairs to get ready for the day. It hadn't sunk in yet that she would not get to see Elliot again, she wouldn't get to hold his hand or kiss him again. Eventually that pain would hit her and she would be utterly heartbroken but for now she had to get ready to pick Katie up from the station. She also had Arnold's ultimatum to consider.

CHAPTER TWENTY

The drive to the station was peaceful. Prue concentrated on the road in front of her and every time her mind strayed she forced herself to think of Katie and her plans for the bookshop over the coming days. There was lots to do to keep her busy and distracted. Prue was looking forward to spending some time with Katie, she needed a friend right now. The station was located in one of the neighbouring towns and took about half an hour to get there. Thankfully, it was a dull but dry day and so Prue's Mini was happily trundling along the winding country lanes. Every now and then Elliot's face threatened to encroach on her thoughts but she pushed him to the back of her mind. Just as she had refocused on the road in front of her Prue's phone beeped from her bag in the passenger footwell, it would be another text from Elliot. He had been trying to get hold of her for the past two hours. As much as Prue wanted to give in and pull over to answer the phone she knew that this was how things were suppose to end. They were a carbon copy of her own parents, their fate was doomed and so it was easier they ended things now before life got too complicated.

Eventually, the phone went quiet again and Prue relaxed slightly, she wasn't far from the station now. The final leg of the journey involved busier roads, which required Prue to concentrate on what was going on rather than listening out for her phone.

As she pulled into a parking spot in the station carpark Prue glanced at her phone to see that she was ten minutes early. It was better than being late. With a newfound sense of bravery

Prue grabbed her phone and scrolled through the messages that Elliot had been sending her. He was confused and hurt by her words and was begging her to reconsider. It hurt to read his messages, telling her that he had thought they had a future together. It was exactly how Prue had felt until reality had hit her. Sooner or later he would realise why she did it and know that it was for the best. One day he would thank her for having the courage to end things now.

Prue was soon distracted from the thoughts that were whizzing around her head at a hundred miles per hour. A knock on the car window made her jump and drop her phone. As she looked up she saw Katie peering in at her with a huge grin on her face. Prue leapt out of the car and flung her arms around her friend, with tears pouring down her face.

'Hey, I haven't aged that much since I last saw you!' Katie tried to make her smile and it worked, she always knew how to change the mood in the room. Or in this case the mood on the pavement, by the side of the car.

'It's been a tough few weeks Kate.' Prue sighed as she pulled back to look at her friend. She looked good, really good. Her friend was dressed in a purple flowing long top that she had thrown on over leggings. Their styles were worlds apart and yet the two girls had just immediately clicked. Katie with her curly red hair and Prue with her sleek dark locks. They were polar opposites and yet their souls recognised each other. As Prue continued to inspect her friend's appearance she felt a pang of jealously as she realised that Katie looked happy.

'Come on, let's get you home and we can have a good catch up.' Somehow they squished Katie's oversized suitcase into the back of the car and they set off back towards the village. As they got nearer and nearer Prue felt the familiar sickening feeling in the pit of her stomach. Having Katie sat beside her was a reminder of her old life and how happy she had once been.

'How's work?' Katie asked, completely unaware of the chaos inside of Prue's head.

'I haven't been working. I've been trying to sort the estate out, prevent an angry mob from torching my home and restoring a bookshop that I discovered my mother had once owned and run.' It came out in a jumble of words with a sob at the end. Prue had been trying to keep her emotions locked up, at least until they had got back and Katie had unpacked.

'Oh Prue, you should have called me sooner.' The sincerity in Katie's tone brought a fresh round of tears to Prue's eyes. Even in the short time that she had been away she had forgotten how close they had been. When Prue left Brighton she had gone with the mindset of starting a new life and leaving her old one behind. With her friend sat next to her Prue now realised that it wasn't a matter of one life or the other, she could have both. At least she could have both providing the villagers would accept her.

Somehow through the tears Prue managed to drive them home and they were soon sitting at the breakfast bar with gin fizzes in front of them. It was technically afternoon and so a gin or two was par for the course. With a box of tissues on hand Prue told Katie everything that had happened since she had left Brighton. Saying it out loud made her realise just how much she had been bottling up, a village full of hate, the revelation about her father and a failed relationship. She had crammed a lot into the short time that she had been home.

'Hold on, let me get this straight. You've broken up with Elliot so that you can find your father?' Katie's eyes were wide as she tried to process all the information.

'Yes but also because his father won't stop harassing me until I do. We'd never work out Kate, it would end in heartbreak and I don't want that. I've just come home, I want a quiet life and some time to settle into my new life.' Even as she said it out loud Prue was still trying to convince herself that she would be better off without Elliot in her life. Since getting home she had turned her phone off and shut it away in a drawer, she only hoped he didn't come round.

'You really like him.' Katie always had the knack of knowing how Prue was feeling, even when she was saying the opposite.

'I really like him Kate but it's just too complicated. It's not worth the hassle when I have so many other things to sort out.' Prue decided to go and fetch the diary from her room so that Katie could read her mother's entries about meeting her father.

'They sounded perfect for each other.' Katie sighed as she closed the diary and carefully placed it on the kitchen worktop.

'That's the terrible thing, they were so happy.'

'Have you read anymore?' Katie asked, leaning forward and squeezing Prue's hand, she could see how upset her friend was.

'No, not yet. I should though, shouldn't I?' Prue had been reluctant to pick the diary back up and read any more. She wanted to treasure the memory of their first date and leave them in their bubble of happiness. The remainder of the day was spent drinking copious amounts of gin and somehow setting fire to a ready meal that they had put in the oven. As they rolled about laughing Prue couldn't help but yearn for her old life in Brighton. It was too late now though, she had made the decision to come home and home was where she was staying. With Katie by her side Prue knew that the next week would feel that bit easier. It was time she settled herself into the village and got on with her life.

That night in bed Prue picked up the diary from her bedside table and began to flick through the pages. She didn't want to read about her parent's relationship but she did want to read about the grand opening of the bookshop. Prue was busy planning the shop's re-opening and so she was interested to read about how its original opening had gone. Eventually, Prue found the page that she had been looking for.

◆ ◆ ◆

14th July 1994

I did it! Today was the grand opening of The Vintage Bookshop of Memories. I got to the shop early this morning and just stood in the doorway peering in. It felt like a dream.

The shop looks like it's just fallen out of one of the novels inside. Robert has done an amazing job with the balcony and he even sourced an antique ladder to access it. He also surprised me with a new counter and in pride of place on top was an old fashioned cash register. I'd told Robert that it was my dream to have one and so he went out and got one for me.

Diary, I'm sure you're sick of hearing about Robert so I promise to only tell you about the bookshop launch today.

As I stood in the doorway looking in at my own little slice of heaven I felt the excitement bubble up inside of me. Mother has helped me market the shop in other villages and nearby towns as she suspects nobody from Ivy Hatch will turn up. I don't care if they turn up or not. In fact, I think I'd rather they didn't, then they wouldn't be able to tarnish my little shop. I hate them all. Today isn't a day to be thinking about them though, today is about me and my little bookshop.

I stayed up all night baking butterfly cupcakes and so when I got to the shop I laid them out on the big table. The table had once stood in the middle of our hallway at the manor, however I persuaded mother to donate it to the shop. Today, it's adorned with cakes and my favourite books - the perfect combination.

Both mother and Robert are going to be with me today, they're both concerned about me spending all day on my feet working. Sometimes I get so fed up of having a weak heart. I can't complain though because it has fallen in love with Robert and in my eyes it's fulfilled its role. Oh here I go again, talking about Robert.

Anyway, the day was a dream. We played jazz music in the background, as lots of people I didn't recognise came in and out of the shop, many of them buying books. Everyone commented on the little notes that I had popped inside and said they'd be back soon to buy my recommendation. The atmosphere in the shop made me want to burst with happiness. The stories of each book were bursting out of the pages and reflecting on the customer's faces. There was pure joy on everyone's face as they treated themselves to a little parcel filled with an alternative world.

Only one person from the village came in, her name was Maggie. Maggie and I were once very good friends but that seems like a lifetime ago now. She was lovely and we sat and talked for a few minutes about our favourite books. She was afraid to buy anything in case her husband discovered where she had been but she promised to come back soon and like everyone else, she left with a big smile on her face.

The residents of Ivy Hatch don't like me and so they're avoiding the shop. Today was obvious but it doesn't upset me in the slightest. My shop will be a safer place without them frequenting it.

I'm exhausted after all the excitement today. I can't wait to spend everyday in my little bookshop as people come in and out to buy their books.

Goodnight diary.

CHAPTER TWENTY ONE

After reading her mother's diary entry Prue had considered delaying the launch of the bookshop. She wanted it to be perfect and to honour her mother's memory, however she was worried that given the village's opinion of her the day could be ruined. Katie had pointed out how unhelpful that would be towards her getting on with her life and so Prue decided to be brave and re-launch the little shop. With this in mind the two girls dedicated the week to getting the little shop ready for its Saturday launch. Thankfully, Elliot had left her alone, the one time they had bumped into each other in the village Katie had been completely oblivious and kept chatting away, giving Prue the perfect excuse to ignore him. She knew it was harsh but she had to do it, she had to show him that she didn't care so that he could walk away. Inside, her heart was breaking all over again. She had to keep reminding herself that the pain would be worth it once she was settled into the village and a part of the community. She would have her home again and then she could start considering a relationship, just not with Elliot.

The bookshop was looking amazing. Katie had designed posters and they had put them up around town and even dropped a few off at the cafe. Over the past week the new contracts had been rolled out and the villagers seemed happier, at least there had been less hateful glares towards Prue. Yesterday the pub landlord had even offered her a drink on the house the next time she popped in. It was strange yet gratifying to see the shift in their attitude towards her.

It was now the morning of the launch and the girls woke early to set everything up. The table in the centre of the shop sat proudly, still with the war theme. Prue had asked the villagers for some pictures of local soldiers and they had complied. The pictures sat proudly on the table surrounded by cupcakes made at the local cafe. The cakes were a nod towards the shop's first open day, however Prue had opted not to bake them herself, she didn't need anyone sampling her baking. Prue was proud of her hard work, the place looked amazing and she couldn't wait to share it. Katie had suggested they promote the shop on one of the local radio stations and so on Wednesday they had driven to the studio and been interviewed about *The Vintage Bookshop of Memories*. It had been lots of fun and had generated quite a bit of interest. Prue only hoped that the few people in the village that still held a grudge against her didn't ruin the day.

Prue hadn't seen Arnold since he had come to the manor and for that she was very thankful. She didn't think she could face him right now, at least not without turning into an emotional mess. She was still incredibly angry over his actions. There was a part of Prue that was willing Elliot to come today, she wanted to see his face again and for him to see what she had done with the shop. Deep down she knew it was a silly dream and that seeing him wouldn't do any good, it would only make not seeing him harder. She couldn't help it though, she missed him, even after such a short time knowing him. There was a gap in her life where he had been. He had made her smile and comforted her when she had nobody else around and she had repaid him by being so cruel and cold hearted.

'Stop it.' Katie whispered in her ear. Prue jumped and turned to look at her friend, how had she known what she had been thinking about?

'You had that wistful look on your face again.' Katie replied and shrugged her shoulders.

Prue couldn't dwell on it as her first customers had just walked into the shop and she went over to greet them. It was Mr and Mrs Burrows who owned the village shop, which sold everything from apples to wool.

'Thank you for coming.' Prue beamed at them, as she walked towards them.

'This place hasn't changed a bit.' Mrs Burrows gasped as she glanced around.

'You remember it?' Prue asked. From her limited interaction with the village everyone had remained silent about the history of the shop, all pretending they didn't know about its existence.

'Of course I remember it. This was your mother's pride and joy.' It brought tears to Prue's eyes to hear someone speaking so fondly of her mother and of the bookshop. This reaction was not one Prue was accustomed to.

'I hope she would be proud of what I've done with it.' Prue's voice wobbled a little as she thought about what her mother might think of the shop.

'She'd love it dear.' Mrs Burrows took Prue's hand in hers and gave it a quick squeeze before moving out the way so that others could enter the shop.

The day was a success, most of the village and lots of people from further afield popped in to see *The Vintage Bookshop of Memories*. Everyone was so kind and lovely, Prue almost felt as though the last few weeks had been a bad dream. Seeing everybody coming together today and being so friendly made her feel like the struggles to win the village over had been worth it. Of course, there were still a few people that were unhappy with the outcome but they were now in the minority.

As the day whizzed by and Prue spoke to everyone, she couldn't help but keep an eye out for Elliot. She didn't catch a single glimpse of him. However, his mother did pop in. Prue made sure she kept her distance and allowed Katie to welcome the woman and offer her any assistance. It would be too painful to speak to her, to look into the eyes that mirrored Elliot's. She had enough to contend with today without the heartache and longing for him. Once Elliot's mother had left and Prue threw herself back into the event at hand she found herself soon smiling again. There was something contagious about the atmosphere within this shop, it was as if all the happiness from the books were seeping out and casting their spell on the unknowing occupants.

Every time a book sold Prue couldn't help but think about the little note that would be stowed away inside. Her mother's handwriting that she would never see again. A part of her had wanted to take the note out of each book and keep them but she knew that the handwritten recommendation was part of the bookshop's charm. It was something she intended to continue and it was only right that the little piece of her mother remained inside the books.

'That was amazing!' Katie exclaimed as they shut the door behind their last customer. It had been one hell of a day.

'I can't believe how well it went. Some of the villagers were positively nice to me!'

'I think you're going to be very happy here Prudence.' Katie giggled as she threw an arm around Prue's shoulders. Prue rolled her eyes at Katie's use of her full name, only her grandmother had ever called her by it.

'Shall we try the local pub for dinner? There's no way I'm going in there alone so we're going to have to go at some point while you're here.' Plus Prue really didn't feel like cooking after such a busy day.

The girls agreed and so after a quick clean and tidy they grabbed their coats and off they went. Stowed away at the bottom of Prue's bag was a new book, she had spotted it in the course of the day and decided to treat herself. It was a romance based in the eighteenth century and looked like it was just the kind of book to snuggle down with after a long day. As much as Prue was looking forward to dinner she couldn't wait until she was in bed with a cup of tea and her book. For now though she wanted to live in the moment, tomorrow was Katie's last day with her and she wanted to make the most of her company.

With some trepidation Prue pushed open the door to the pub and both girls walked in. Every head turned but unlike last time there were a few smiles and nods towards them. It was bizarre having gone from such extremes, to be hated by an entire village then to suddenly feel accepted by them. Prue had to just accept it though, it would do no good to keep dwelling on it. They made their way over to one of the tables at the back of the pub. It wasn't very busy but the usual locals were in. As they sat down the landlord came over to give them each a menu.

'Well done today Prue, the shop looks amazing. We're glad to have you as part of the community and helping bring tourists into the village to keep our businesses running.' Prue was taken back by his words, she hadn't been expecting such a warm welcome.

'Thank you for giving me the chance to prove myself.' Prue couldn't express how she was feeling in words. She was finally feeling happy to be home.

'I think you're going to be fine here Prue. You just had to be strong and show them that you're here for the duration.' Katie reached across the table and gave Prue's hand a squeeze. Prue would be sad to see Katie go home on Monday but she knew her friend would be back soon. Her visit had been just what Prue had needed, a reminder that she wasn't alone in all of this.

The girls ordered their meals and a bottle of red wine to share. Prue was finally feeling as though she was able to relax. There was the odd glance towards their table and hushed voices but that was something Prue would have to learn to live with. She owned the majority of the village so someone would always have an opinion on her. Despite the few glances Prue was getting she felt as though there were another pair of eyes on her but she couldn't locate them, it was beginning to send a chill down her spine.

'Katie, is someone behind me staring at me? I feel as though someone's watching me.'

'There's four people at a table behind you, looks like a mother, father, possibly a son and his girlfriend. The son is the one looking at you, he looks around our age. He's really good looking actually, dark hair, dark eyes and some stubble.' Prue felt her heart plummet at the description, it sounded like Elliot. She wondered how she could look without making it obvious.

'Pick up your glass and smile at me.' Katie instructed as she pulled out her phone to take a picture. As much as Prue really didn't want to have her picture taken she did want to see who was staring at her and so she gave in and smiled for the camera.

'Was it a good one?' Prue asked, playing along and reaching across the table to look at the picture. She zoomed in to the table behind her and sure enough there was Elliot sat there, staring towards them. Prue felt her heart constrict as she looked at his face, he looked just the same as he had the last time she had seen him. That wasn't what captured her attention though. Also sat at the table were Elliot's mother, father and a mysterious blonde. The woman looked to be overly friendly with Elliot as she was leaning in to whisper something into his ear. Prue felt sick looking at the picture, it hadn't taken him long to move on. Their relationship may have been short but she had thought it had meant something.

'That's Elliot.' Prue whispered, sliding the phone back across the table. Katie's eyes flashed with recognition and she glanced over at the table again.

'I think they're leaving. Please don't let it spoil your day.'

Prue knew Katie was right, she had worked too hard for today, she couldn't let something so trivial ruin it. Their brief relationship had obviously meant nothing to Elliot and so she shouldn't waste anytime pining over him. It was time her life moved on and she had enough to keep her busy for the time being.

CHAPTER TWENTY TWO

Katie's final day had whizzed by in a blur of laughter and happy tears. They had spent the day at the bookshop again. The customers had kept coming and everyone had something nice to say about the little bookshop. For Prue it was a dream come true to see her mother's legacy living on, with a little help from herself. After a chat with Katie they had agreed that perhaps Prue should consider employing somebody in the shop for a few days a week. Prue had to agree, as much as she loved the shop she also missed her own work. To some working at an auction house may sound boring but to her it was a glimpse into history. She got to handle pieces from people's lives and consider their history and value. There was no better role for Prue. It was something that she would always enjoy and Katie was right, she shouldn't dedicate her entire life to the village or her mother's memory. It had hurt to hear it but Katie had her best interests at heart, Prue had her own life to live.

That was Prue's focus for the coming week to find someone willing to work in the shop and to research some local auction houses. It felt good to have a plan and to know that she finally had her life on some form of track. Katie had encouraged her to keep busy, she suspected that her friend understood just how heartbroken she was under the happy facade. It would be okay though, after all Prue was only just re-building her life, she had a long way to go yet.

On Monday morning Prue dropped Katie back at the station and they both shed a few tears as they said goodbye. Katie had promised to visit again soon and Prue knew she would keep her word. With a final goodbye Prue jumped back into her car and began the journey home. The shop was shut today and so she had the day to herself to do whatever she wanted. She knew she should begin on her list of tasks but she didn't feel like it today. After such a busy week there was nothing Prue wanted more than to curl up with the book that she had brought home from the shop on Saturday. She hadn't had the chance to even open it yet, Saturday night she had cried herself to sleep after seeing Elliot at the pub.

Once back at the manor Prue made herself a cup of tea and took her book into the library. The worn sofas may not have looked very pretty but they were comfortable and so she grabbed one of the fur throws and curled up with her book. She was ready to immerse herself in someone else's life.

As she opened the book a piece of paper fell out, expecting to see her mother's handwriting Prue picked it up and unfolded it. However, to her surprise it wasn't her mother's handwriting that she was looking at. She wasn't quite sure whose it was and so she began to read the letter.

Dear Dottie,

I wonder how long it's taken you to find this note. I suspect it won't take you long to realise there's a rogue book on your shelves. You live and breathe those books.

I'm sorry for the trouble I've caused. I hope your mother can forgive you one day for falling in love with a 'commoner' like me. I thought you would appreciate the irony of me placing the note inside of this book - it's a forbidden romance set in the eighteenth-century between a princess and one of her servants.

There's no work for me here, the villagers have made sure of that. Nobody within a 50 mile radius will hire me. They all think I'm stepping out of line and trying to better myself. They don't realise that it's as simple as having fallen in love with the wrong girl.

I'm rambling and I know you hate it when I do that so I'll get to the point. I have to leave for a while. I'm going to try and find some work, hopefully nearby. Once I have something permanent I'll be in touch and we can be together again.

I love you Dottie, even though I shouldn't.

I'll love you forever.

Yours always,
Robert

Tears fell from Prue's eyes and hit the piece of paper in her hands, so much for losing herself in someone else's world. This letter had been written by her father to her mother. Prue turned the paper over in her hands, it looked as though her mother had never found the letter. It broke Prue's heart to know how much her father had loved her mother and yet he had been driven away because the village's archaic views on life. No wonder Prue's grandmother had been so harsh, having to sit back and watch her little girl's heart be broken beyond repair. Prue's grandmother had always hidden her emotions, it was what made it so difficult to feel close to her. However, Prue had never doubted that she was loved and it was clear from her grandmother's actions that she had loved her daughter.

With a sudden jolt, Prue realised she could read her mother's diary to discover whether she had ever read the letter. She needed to know what had happened and whether her mother had ever been in contact with her father again. The note from

Robert was dated and so Prue flicked through the diary to the date and began reading. The closest entry was dated the following day.

18th April 1995

He's gone. I've looked everywhere for him but there's no sign, his belongings have gone from the B&B he was staying at and nobody has seen him. Although I doubt anyone would tell me if they had. I hate this village and everyone in it, how dare they try to control my life like this. They view us as a different class of people just because we own land, it's utterly ridiculous.

I will never forgive them.

I tried to go to the shop today but I couldn't even open the door. I knew that as soon as I went in my mind would be flooded with memories of us. The bookshop will never be the same.

Oh diary, I don't know what to do without him. I feel as though I'll never smile again.

19th April 1995

He's definitely gone. What am I going to do without him? Robert understood every part of me and I thought we had our lives planned. In two weeks time we're suppose to be going travelling. Nobody knows about our plans, perhaps he'll be back and he'll take me away with him. Away from all of them.

Mother is furious. She said I never should have fallen for him. I've been promised to the Devon's son since birth and I've ruined it all. She thought it was just a phase that I was going through but I think tonight she realised just how much I love Robert.

Prue had to put the diary down for a second as she processed everything that she had just read. It was difficult to read her mother's heartbreak and to know how pointless it was. To separate two people who were in love just because of a perceived class. It had also shocked Prue to read her mother's reference to an arranged marriage. Prue knew of the Devon family, the land that wasn't owned by the Clemontes was owned by them. The arranged marriage must have been a business deal to merge the families and to own all of the surrounding land. No wonder her mother had wanted to fall in love with whomever she pleased. That was why the villagers had been so angry that she and Robert had fallen in love. The Devons had been trying to poach Ivy Hatch's land for years and so a marriage between the families would signify an alliance. Despite this, Prue knew it didn't make any of their actions right. How selfish they had been to expect her mother to marry for the benefit of the village.

As Prue opened the diary again she noticed that there was only one more entry from 1995. She took a deep breath before she read her mother's last words.

5th May 1995

Well diary, it's true he's gone for good. Our plans to go travelling must have meant nothing to him. I waited at the end of the gate for him, just as we had planned. I was sure he would still come and we would make our way to France. By the time I went back inside I was shivering from the cold and with tears running down my face. He's moved on with his life and mother says I must too. How can I move on though when I'm having his child? Mother doesn't know yet, I'm dreading telling her. The village will no doubt have something to say about it but it's not their baby, it's mine.

I've decided that I have to try and move on with my life. It's too painful for me to keep the bookshop open and so after writing this I'm going to lock the doors for the last time. Life will continue on the outside but our relationship will be trapped in these four walls, the memories of our meeting and our short-lived dates will forever stay in this building.

Perhaps our child will discover the shop one day.

Goodbye Robert.

Prue almost felt as though her mother was sat beside her as she read the words she had written all those years ago. It was heart-breaking to read how upset her mother had been. Prue was also confused as to what had happened. Why had her father never tried to get in contact again? It looked as though her mother had never found the letter that he had left in the bookshop. There were so many unanswered questions. Prue needed to know the truth and she wanted to know it soon. There was only one person that could help her, he was the last person in the world she wanted to see but Prue knew she had to be brave and talk to him. Prue had to go and see Arnold Harrington.

CHAPTER TWENTY THREE

The following morning Prue took her time getting ready, not because she wanted to make the effort but because she was dreading going to see Arnold. She had no way of contacting him and so she had decided her best option was to just turn up at the farm and hope that Elliot wasn't there, it was unlikely but she was still worried. Prue opted for a pair of navy waist high sailor trousers and a matching stripy top. Prue would have to be quick as she had to get back in time for an online book auction. She knew she had to leave soon and yet she was still dragging her heels.

With a resentful sigh Prue left the manor and began the short drive to the Harrington's farm. She hadn't ever been there and yet she owned it. Prue still found it a little strange that she owned all of the land that she could see, it was somewhat surreal. Thankfully the farm was signposted off of the main road. Prue turned onto an unmade road and crossed her fingers as her Mini struggled over all of the potholes. Finally, Prue pulled up outside a farm house and breathed a sigh of relief. The house looked inviting with an orange light glowing through the window, smoke billowing from the chimney and the sound of cows mooing in the background. It looked real and homely, something that Prue was yearning for right now.

'What do you want?' Prue whirled around to see who was shouting at her. The man had just emerged from one of the barns on the other side of the courtyard. Prue's heart gave a little thud as she took in the man's appearance, he was Elliot's double.

'I'm looking for your father.' Prue replied, standing up taller, she refused to be intimidated by her own tenants.

'He doesn't want to see you.' The man started walking across the courtyard towards one of the fields, indicating that the conversation was over.

'I suggest you go and get your father. He's yet to sign the new contract and I'm well within my rights to terminate the agreement. Unless he wants to lose the farm you best go and tell him that Miss Clemonte wants to speak to him.' Prue saw the flash of anger across the young man's face. She knew what she had just said would only anger the family but she didn't know how else to get through to them that she wanted to speak.

'Go and wait inside, my mother's there.' With that the man stalked off into one of the neighbouring fields.

The last thing Prue wanted was to sit in a small room with Elliot's mother and so she edged towards her car, she would sit in there until Arnold came. However, just as Prue's hand landed on the car door's handle the farmhouse's door opened and Elliot's mother stood there staring at her.

'You better come in.' She said, holding the door wide open for Prue. Rather reluctantly Prue made her way into the house and found herself in a large kitchen with a huge solid wooden table in the centre. The aga was on with a kettle in pride of place on the top, with steam pouring out of it. On the other side of the room was a roaring fire and a heap of dogs lying in front of it. There was something very inviting and cosy about the room, despite the icy reception that Prue had received. A fleeting thought passed through Prue's head, she could live here if she wanted. The Harringtons hadn't signed the contract yet. It wouldn't be the same though, she would be on her own in the middle of nowhere with a million cows to look after. Well, maybe not a million but still she could barely look after a succulent let alone an entire farm.

'Would you like a tea or coffee?' Elliot's mother broke the silence as she gestured to Prue to sit down at the table.

'Could I have a cup of coffee please?' It came out as a question as Prue found herself feeling a little out of place in the presence of such a motherly figure. There was something about the woman that made Prue feel five years old again.

In a flash the woman had made a coffee and had sat opposite Prue with her own mug in her hand.

'What are you doing here, Prudence?' Prue was taken aback at the woman's use of her full name, she had become accustomed to the village referring to her as 'Miss Clemonte'.

'I'm sorry for imposing myself on you without any notice Mrs Harrington. I've just come to ask your husband a few questions.'

'Please call me Maggie. Are these questions in relation to the farm?' A worried look flashed across the woman's face and Prue immediately felt guilty about using the farm as ammunition to get Arnold to speak to her.

'No Maggie, I promise you I won't be forcing you into any decisions about the farm. This is your home and if you choose to sign the new contract and stay here then that's completely up to you. I don't want to throw anyone out of their home, I just want to be a part of village life and walk down the street without constant hateful glares.' Prue was taken back by the sudden rush of emotion as she spoke to Maggie. She really just wanted to feel at home in the village again.

'Your mother was just the same as you, until…' Maggie broke off mid sentence and a strange look crossed her face.

'Until what, Maggie?' Prue questioned, although she suspected she knew the answer. If she were right then Maggie was about to refer to her mother and father's relationship.

'Oh nothing dear, would you like some breakfast?' The woman jumped up and began to busy herself with some pots and pans on the aga.

'Maggie, did you mean until my father left?'

Maggie turned around from her place at the aga and her eyes darted nervously towards the door.

'Yes. Until then. Prue, your mother and I were good friends. Arnold never knew, he wouldn't have approved of me befriending somebody from above our class. I'm afraid this village is stuck in the past, I only hope you can help to modernise it.'

Silence fell in the kitchen as the sound of footsteps crossing the courtyard echoed throughout.

'Maggie, come and visit me at the bookshop later in the week. I'd love to speak to you.' Prue whispered just before the kitchen door swung open and Arnold stood there looking like he was about to burst with anger.

'You're not taking my farm away from me!' He shouted, sitting down opposite Prue and slamming his fists down on the table.

'Arnold, I don't intend to take the farm away from you. I trust you received the new contract, please take your time to read through it and get back to me. I'm here about my father.'

Arnold looked visibly jumpy as Prue brought up the topic of her father.

'Maggie, go and feed the hens.' There was no politeness in his tone, he wanted Maggie outside before they spoke. Prue cast a final glance towards Maggie as she slipped out of the kitchen doorway with a basket in hand.

'I assume you've kept to your side of the bargain?' Arnold questioned, getting up from the table and walking over to the mantlepiece above the burning fire.

'I've not seen or spoken to Elliot for over a week.' It saddened Prue to say it out loud but she had to keep telling herself it was for the best. At least this way she would find her father and Elliot wouldn't have the opportunity to break her heart. Besides, Elliot had moved on already, that had been clear when she had seen him at the pub.

'Here's his address.' Arnold handed Prue a folded up piece of paper that he had taken from an envelope on the mantlepiece.

'How do you have his address?' Prue asked, confused as to why a man who wanted to uphold social status would be in contact with the man who almost brought it all crashing down.

'I have a conscience. As much as I didn't agree with your mother and father's relationship a child should grow up with their parents.' As Prue let those words sink in the cogs in her brain began to turn. Did that mean...?

'Arnold, does my father know about me?' The silence in the room was deafening as Prue watched a range of emotions flicker across Arnold's face as he tried to decide how to answer her question.

'He does. Over the years I've written to him to give him a little update on your life. It's been a few years since I sent the last letter but he's always kept me up to date with where he's living.'

Prue didn't know quite what to do with this new information. If her father knew about her existence then why had he never come looking for her? That meant he must have known about her mother's death and so why hadn't he come to meet his daughter? A sinking feeling in the pit of Prue's stomach began to make her feel sick. Perhaps he didn't want anything to do with her.

'Thank you.' Prue whispered, she pushed the folded up piece of paper into her pocket and turned on her heel to exit.

'He did love your mother Prue. It was just unfortunate that this village has a way of doing things and their relationship went against that.'

Without turning round Prue left the house with Arnold's final words echoing throughout her head.

CHAPTER TWENTY FOUR

Prue was not quite sure how she made it to the bookshop, all she knew was that ten minutes after leaving the Harrington's farm she was unlocking the door to the shop. A million and one thoughts were buzzing around her head and she didn't know where to start to process them. Prue decided that a cup of tea was the most logical place to start. She made herself a cup in one of her vintage tea cups and then brought it out into the shop. It was a cold but sunny day and so she opened the door to the shop and left it wedged open slightly, to let some fresh air in, she only hoped that nobody thought she was open. Katie had got hold of a chalkboard sign for her and had painted '*The Vintage Bookshop of Memories*' onto it, Prue brought the sign inside. The last thing she wanted was to see anyone right now.

With a cup of tea in hand Prue took her seat behind the counter and began to sift through the endless thoughts in her head. She really ought to be grabbing her laptop from her bag and logging into the online auction, however her mind was too jumbled to focus on anything. It had been quite a bombshell to hear that her father knew of her existence. All along Prue had assumed he couldn't know about her or else he would have been in her life. This time last year Prue was happy and living her life in Brighton with not a single care about her father, so why did he matter to her now? Perhaps it was the sudden realisation that she had no family left.

Eventually Prue focused herself and logged onto the online auction. She opted to make herself feel better by buying tonnes of books. Who said retail therapy wasn't real therapy? Once the auction was over Prue couldn't face going back home with her thoughts and so she decided to open the bookshop. To distract herself she began to pull books off their shelf to read her mother's note inside of them. Once read she would replace the note back inside the book and slide them back into their spot. The memories that this little shop held were incredible, Prue only wished that each book could speak and tell her their story, everything that they had seen and heard over the years.

As lunchtime approached Prue heard footsteps along the cobbled street leading up to the shop. She was grateful to have a customer to distract herself before she started sobbing over the heartbreak that this shop had witnessed. Prue watched in horror as Elliot pushed the door open and walked into the shop. Thankfully there were no other customers and no villagers to spread rumours about his visit.

'What do you want?' Prue asked, her tone was a little harsher than she meant it to be but she'd had a stressful morning and seeing Elliot was the last thing she needed.

'I came to see you.' He shrugged, looking a little taken back at her attitude towards him. Prue almost felt herself feeling sorry for him but then she remembered how quickly he had moved on with the blonde in the pub.

'Well you've seen me so now you can go.' Now she had adopted this standoffish tone Prue couldn't stop and if she was honest with herself she just wanted him to leave. She really didn't need the added stress.

'Don't be like this Prue. At the very least I think I deserve an explanation, you did dump me by text after all.'

Prue was starting to feel angry, how dare he come here and have a go at her! He was the one whose dysfunctional family had tormented her life since coming back to the village. It was also his father that had been writing to her father and had told him about her existence.

'Excuse me for thinking you didn't care when you've already moved on with another woman. I'd like you to leave now please.' Prue stood up from behind the counter and made her way round towards Elliot in an attempt to herd him towards the door.

'You're too caught up in the past, that's your problem, Prue. Your head is constantly stuck reliving other people's lives, rather than your own, even your dress sense is from another era. You need to live your life Prue and stop comparing it to the past. Memories are something to look back on, you have to live in the present to create them. You're far too busy living in other people's memories to make any of your own.'

Prue hadn't been expecting those words to come from Elliot's mouth. Yes, she liked history, after all she wouldn't be a very good at her job if she didn't. She also enjoyed dressing in 1940's clothes. It didn't mean she was obsessed with the past, did it? She just had an appreciation for memories and keeping past times alive. There was nothing wrong in honouring the past.

'I think you better leave Elliot, now.' The anger on both of their faces was apparent, each of them using the emotion to cloak the heartbreak that they were truly feeling.

Without uttering another word Elliot left the shop and Prue slammed the door shut behind him, locking the door to ensure he couldn't return. How dare he barge into her shop and accuse her of living in the past. A tiny part of Prue's brain started to question whether he had a point. The entire village was living in the past, it was how she had been brought up. Perhaps she needed to reconsider her outlook on life and start looking more towards future, rather than the past. Although those thoughts did make some sense Prue angrily pushed them away. She would not accept that Elliot had a point. He had shown himself to be just like his father, rude and judgmental and she would be happy if she never set eyes on him again.

CHAPTER TWENTY FIVE

The next couple of days passed in a blur as Prue stuck to her daily routine of working at the shop all day, going home and having dinner and then going straight to bed. Katie had tried calling her a couple of times but she had ignored her, allowing each call to go to voicemail. She knew at some point she would have to return her calls, it would be cruel to leave Katie worrying, but for now Prue didn't want to speak to anyone. Working in the shop all day was exhausting as she tried to hide the upset and anger that was bubbling away inside of her. The only upside was that the villagers were all supporting the bookshop and were regularly popping in and making purchases. It gave Prue hope for the future. She almost felt like texting Elliot and pointing out that she was looking towards the future not the past. She didn't though, it would be petty and she knew it would only anger her more when he didn't reply.

Prue was focusing on just getting through each day and to her relief every time she woke up she found herself feeling a little less unhappy. Every now and then thoughts about her father crept into her mind and she couldn't help but wonder what he was doing at that moment in time. Last night Prue had held the piece of paper in her hand and stared down at it. She contemplated sending him a letter but she knew she wouldn't be satisfied with just a letter. If he didn't want anything to do with her then she wanted to hear that from him, face-to-face, at least that way she would have met him and would have a face to put to the memories.

It was Friday morning and Prue was browsing some online book auctions to restock the shelves. She loved second-hand books, all she could think about was how many other people had held them and rejoiced in the pages. They held so many memories. Yet again, Prue found herself wishing that the books could speak, she was fascinated to know what they had seen and who they had been held by. Perhaps she was a little obsessed with the past but there was nothing wrong with that. She preferred to think of it as an appreciation, rather than an obsession.

The door opened and Prue looked up with her best customer worthy smile but she was taken-aback to see Maggie stood in the doorway looking a little apprehensive.

'Maggie! Please come in.' Prue stood up from her seat behind the counter and flapped her arms, not really sure what to do to encourage the woman to come in.

'Thank you, dear. I can't be long as I have only popped out for a loaf of bread but I just wanted to stop by and see how you were doing.' The woman walked into the shop and closed the door behind her. She was looking very smart today dressed in a pair of green jeans and a brown wax Barbour jacket, her dark hair was pulled back into a low pony tail.

'I'm doing really well, thank you.' Prue replied in an overly happy tone. Maggie immediately gave her a reproving look and made her way towards the comfortable leather chair and took a seat.

'Why don't you make us both a cup of tea and we can have a little chat.' The way Maggie said it reminded her of the assurance that both Elliot and his father had. Prue knew that there would be no way out of this little chat and so she went to put the kettle on.

'Why are you really here, Maggie?' Prue asked as she stood in the doorway to the kitchenette waiting for the kettle to boil.

'I spoke to Elliot yesterday and he told me about what happened when he came round the other day. I told him off Prue, I don't think he was right to accuse you of living in the past.'

Unsure what to say in response Prue nipped back into the kitchenette and made their drinks, giving herself enough time to compose her features and stop herself from giving too much away.

'You said you were friends with my mother?' Prue sat back down behind the counter and prompted Maggie to start talking, whilst also distracting her from asking questions about Elliot.

'We were. When we were little we would play together around the village. I'm a few years older than your mum but that didn't matter. We had great fun foraging around the fields and your grandad would take us for drives in his convertible car.' Prue never got to meet her grandad as he had died when her mother was only fifteen.

'How comes you grew apart?' Prue asked, she was always eager to hear people's memories of her mother. It was like she had the opportunity to get to know her all over again.

'I married Arnold when I turned eighteen and our lives went in different directions. Your mother went off to study at university, meanwhile I was busy helping Arnold to keep the farm afloat. As you know the village aren't keen on social classes mixing and so our friendship was never encouraged. I think things have improved since you came back Prue. The villagers see you as a part of the community rather than an outsider who owns everything in sight.' It was reassuring to hear Maggie speak of her being accepted into village life.

'That's what I want Maggie. I want to be a part of the village life. I grew up here, this is my home.'

'You want to find your father, too.' Maggie wasn't asking a question, it was a statement.

'Yes, I do. I've never really thought about him but now I know of his existence and the part he played in my mother's life I feel as though I must meet him. It's like a chapter in a book, I have to finish it even if I don't like the outcome.'

'Prue, be careful. Your father was heartbroken when he had to leave your mother and I think he's built a lot of walls up to protect himself. He may not be the loving father you want.' Maggie's warning shocked Prue, she hadn't even began to consider how her father might have felt. In her eyes he had made the decision to leave her mother but perhaps he hadn't felt like he had a choice. With a sudden realisation Prue remembered how she had justified breaking up with Elliot - it was for the best, for both of them. Perhaps she was more like her father than she had ever realised.

'I have to know Maggie. I can't go through the rest of my life always wondering exactly why he left and why he chose to never come back. At the very least I must try to find out why he didn't fight for my mum and why he never came back for me.' The desperation in Prue's tone was obvious.

'Then you must go in search of him.' With that Maggie stood up and placed her empty cup down on the counter and made her way towards the door.

'Thank you for stopping by.' Prue called after her, she was genuinely feeling a little bit happier after speaking to Maggie.

'I'll come back soon. Prue, give Elliot another chance. You're strong enough to change the village's way of thinking, if you want to. Don't stop yourself from being happy.'

The words hung in the air as Maggie left, shutting the door firmly behind her. Prue really didn't know how she felt about

Elliot anymore, she was beyond confused. Right now she had to focus on making a decision about finding her father. Her feelings towards Elliot had to be buried for the time being. Besides, it didn't matter how she felt, he had made his feelings very clear both through his words and his actions by moving on.

CHAPTER TWENTY SIX

It wasn't until the weekend that Prue felt the loneliness sink in. She'd always been happy in her own company but right now she was longing for someone to come along and distract her from life. It was Saturday morning and she was sat behind the counter in the bookshop watching customers come and go, some would buy a book, others would just browse. It was nice to see the place buzzing with people and yet it only emphasised her loneliness. Only last week Katie had been by Prue's side for the opening of the bookshop and yet here she was, a week later, feeling completely alone. The piece of paper with her father's address on was in her pocket, she hadn't let it out of her sight since Arnold had given it to her. Prue knew that sooner or later she would contact him. She had too many unanswered questions and a part of her yearned for a parent.

'Are you okay dear?' Prue pulled herself away from her pity party and focused on who was stood in front of her. It was Mrs Edwards, one of the elderly ladies from the village. When Prue was a child Mrs Edwards ran the tea rooms and even then she seemed ancient. These days the elderly woman rented one of the Clemonte's cottages and lived in solitude since her husband's death five years ago.

'Sorry, I was just a little distracted.' Prue looked at the pile of books on the counter in front of her and began the process of ringing them up on the old fashioned till.

'It's lovely to see this place open again. You know your mother met your father here.' The statement shocked Prue into looking up. How did this woman know so much about her parents? Everyone else in the village avoided the topic of her parents and yet here Mrs Edwards was openly discussing them.

'You knew my father?' Prue asked, her hands frozen in mid air.

'I did, he's my nephew.'

Prue didn't know what to say or do. The woman stood opposite her was family. She had been living in the same village her entire life and yet Prue never knew that they were related.

'Mrs Edwards, could I speak to you about my father?' Prue's voice was hoarse, she could scarcely believe that she had met somebody who was related to her father.

'Of course you can dear, why don't you drop those books off tonight and come in for a slice of cake and a chat?'

They agreed that Prue would go round once she had closed the shop and with that Mrs Edwards went home to bake a cake. Prue felt somewhat dazed by what had just happened. Mrs Edwards was family and yet nobody had ever told her, had her grandmother even known? It was all too much to comprehend on a Saturday morning with only one cup of coffee coursing through her veins.

Somehow, Prue made it to the end of the day with only a handful of mishaps. She breathed a sigh of relief once she locked the door behind her last customer of the day. It had definitely been one of the longest days she had ever experienced. Prue decided she would tidy the shop the following morning and so she grabbed Mrs Edward's books and made her way to her cottage. It was a short walk as she only lived on the other side of the village green.

The cottage was small but sweet with a brick path up to a wooden stable door. It was incredibly picturesque and looked like a very happy place to live. With a light tremble Prue knocked on the front door and waited for an answer. She didn't know what to expect from their impending conversation, all she knew was that she was about to spend an hour or two with a family member. Somebody that knew her father. It was a daunting prospect and yet excitement was also fizzing up inside of Prue.

The door swung open and Mrs Edwards stood there, she had changed into a smart summer dress with little butterflies covering it. Her grey hair had been neatly curled into a halo around her head and there was a smattering of makeup on her face. Prue smiled to herself at the effort the woman had gone to for their slice of cake and a chat. Despite their difference in social standing, her grandmother would have approved.

'Hello dear, come on in.' She stepped aside to allow Prue into the little house. The inside was just as quaint as the outside. Prue found herself walking directly into the little living room. It was small but cosy with two pale pink sofas and a coffee table with a lace tablecloth over it. On top of the table proudly sat a cake stand with a Victoria sponge cake in the middle of it. To say it looked mouth-wateringly delicious would be an understatement.

'I brought your books Mrs Edwards, where would you like them?' Prue looked around for a suitable place to put them but every surface was either covered in picture frames or knick-knacks.

'Call me Carol, after all we are family. I'll take them from you and pop them on my shelf in the kitchen. You take a seat and I'll be back in a minute with a pot of tea.'

Prue went to offer her help but the look on Carol's face told her not to and so instead she took a seat on one of the pink sofas and waited for the woman to return. There was something comforting about the old-fashioned style of the cottage.

A few minutes later Carol wandered back in with a pot of tea, two vintage cups and a couple of plates for their cakes, all on a tray. Prue watched in silence as the woman expertly cut two doorstop-sized slices of cake and poured the tea.

'It's nice to have somebody to feed. After all those years running The Tea Room it feels strange to only cook for one these days.' The sadness was evident in Carol's tone and just a glance at her eyes showed the true pain she was feeling. Prue could relate, she knew what it was like to go from being surrounded by people to being left on your own to fend for yourself.

'I wish I had known sooner, that we are family.' Prue couldn't help the wistful tone that had accompanied her words. How different her life might have been if she had known about Carol from the start. All those trips to The Tea Room, to have been served by Carol herself and not knowing that they shared the same blood. Prue was certain she would never learn the truth as to why her grandmother kept so many secrets from her but she was dead now and it was Prue's time to trace her remaining family. There was nobody left to upset. Well, that wasn't strictly true, many of the villagers would most likely be upset to know Prue was trying to track down her father, however their opinion didn't matter to her. If her grandmother had still been alive then Prue knew for sure that she would not have pursued this in fear of upsetting her.

'Your grandmother thought it would be easier for you if you didn't know we were related. As I'm sure you already know, the village was unhappy about your mother and father's relationship. After your mother's death your grandmother took it upon herself to shield you from any further pain or disappointment and so we agreed that we wouldn't speak of your father.' Carol took a sip of her tea whilst Prue digested the information that she had just received. All along she had thought that perhaps her grandmother had kept all this from her because she wanted to uphold their place in society, not once had it occurred to her that she may have been doing it to protect Prue.

'How did you feel about that Carol?' Prue asked as she politely took a bite of the cake in front of her. It was delicious but Prue had completely lost her appetite.

'I was upset of course but I still got to be a part of your life, unlike Robert. You may not have known me but I still got to see you grow up and we even had a chat or two when you came into the cafe.'

The room was silent as Prue took a sip of tea to give herself enough time to compile her thoughts and compose her next question.

'Did my father want to be a part of my life?' It was the question that Prue was most dreading the answer to and so she decided to get it out the way with first. Knowing her father's opinion on their relationship, or lack of, would help her know what other questions to ask.

'Prue your father always wanted to be a part of your life. He didn't find out about your existence until you were eight months old. One morning there was a knock on our front door and it was your father. He had returned to the village for your mother but he knew that your grandmother would not let him into the manor and so he asked to stay with us until he could contact your mum. Of course, I had to sit him down and tell him about you. I remember it like it was yesterday, he had tears of joy running down his face as he asked all about you. He was so happy but then suddenly it was as if reality hit him and he realised that if he was a part of your life the village would never let you be happy. He told me that he had to leave you be and allow you to live your life, your mother too. I'm afraid that was the last time I ever saw Robert. He still sends a Christmas card though, every year. I don't have his address so I can't send him one back.'

Prue felt like her head might explode with all the information that she had just been given. Her father hadn't just forgotten about her mother, he had returned and he had wanted to be with her. He also knew about Prue's existence and from the reaction that Carol described he was happy to have a daughter. Prue found that her desire to meet him was strengthening.

'I think I have his address.' Prue almost whispered it as though it was a secret she wasn't suppose to be sharing. Carol looked shocked but she quickly composed her features.

'What are you going to do with it?'

'I'm going to go and find my father.' It wasn't until that moment Prue knew for sure what she was going to do. She was sure that this was the right thing to do. It was time the village changed and accepted her and her family for who they were.

'Would you like some company?' Carol looked hopeful and in that moment Prue felt her heart expand with gratitude. There was nothing she would love more than some company and some moral support from the closest thing she had to family right now.

'I'd love some company. I have to open the shop tomorrow but shall we go on Monday?'

The two of them made plans to set off to the address on Monday morning. Prue knew that it could end in disappointment but she had to take this step and find out. After all, it could go well and she could find her father and Carol could find her nephew.

CHAPTER TWENTY SEVEN

Monday morning Prue woke with a huge knot of nerves in her stomach. Today was the day, at least she hoped it would be. Prue was trying not to get too excited since she had already had one failed attempt at finding her father. There was still the chance that he would have moved or he might simply not be at home. There were so many 'what ifs?' that if Prue spent too long thinking about them she found her head began to spin out of control and she lost her grip on reality. She had to focus on today, one step at a time and right now she was trying to decide what to wear. Trying being the operative word in this situation. Unfortunately, life didn't come with a handbook that advised on what to wear when meeting your long-lost father for the first time.

With half of her wardrobe discarded on her bed Prue was really struggling to decide which outfit to choose. What did one wear to meet their long-lost father for the first time? She almost Googled it before a purple dress at the back of the wardrobe caught her eye. It was a simple 40s style tea dress in a gorgeous purple fabric but it was so much more than that. When Prue and her grandmother had finally gained the courage to clear out her mother's wardrobe they had taken some of the items of clothing and had them altered. This dress was one of those, it had once been a maxi dress with a gorgeous matching platted belt. The belt had been turned into a headband, however Prue decided against wearing it today with the dress. It was enough to know that she had a piece of her mother with her, the same outfit that her mother had met her father in to discuss the bookshop.

After what seemed like a lifetime Prue was finally ready for the day and she made her way into the village, in her Mini, to pick up Carol. As Prue sat outside Carol's cottage waiting for her to come out she breathed a sigh of relief that her love for vintage didn't extend to mobiles. Prue tapped the address into the SatNav on her phone and set it up in the little holdall attached to the windscreen.

'Good morning dear, you look lovely.' Carol slowly climbed into the car and smoothed down her dress. She had obviously put as much effort into her appearance as Prue had that morning. The excitement was obvious on Carol's face as she turned to look at Prue.

'Are you ready for this?' She asked, reaching over to place a reassuring hand on Prue's arm.

'I think so. What about you Carol, are you ready?'

'I think so. Come on let's go.'

According to the SatNav the journey would take them two hours and so both women were eager to start making their way towards the address. The journey itself was lovely and peaceful as they passed endless fields and forests. Under any other circumstances Prue would have been revelling in the beauty of the area and enjoying every moment of the drive. However, today all she wanted was to arrive at the address and meet her father.

The two women chatted endlessly for the entirety of the two hour drive. Carol asked Prue all about her life in Brighton, what she had studied at university and how she had started working in an auction house. In turn, Carol told Prue about her life and how she had come on holiday to the village at the age of twenty, met her husband and never left. Both were grateful for the distraction as their impending visit grew ever closer with each mile that they drove. Soon enough they passed a little sign welcoming them to the town where Prue's father lived. The town was much busier than their little village and lacked the charm of quaint cottages and old fashioned shops lining the main road. Instead, this town boasted lots of chain shops and even a big name coffee shop. After having immersed herself in village-life, Prue felt almost shocked as she looked around at what she had once considered life's necessities. Prue still remembered the little thrill that went through her whenever she walked through the Lanes with a gingerbread latte in her grasp peering through the windows of all the jewellers. It felt like a million miles away from her life now and yet there was a small part of her that yearned for the hustle and bustle of Brighton. To be lost in a sea of people again.

Prue turned a corner at the top of the main road, which took her onto a residential estate. The SatNav was telling her to take a left hand turning and then her destination would be two hundred yards on her right. Suddenly she felt her heart beat speed up and her hands became sweaty as she gripped the steering wheel. They were so close, it wouldn't be long until she was knocking on a front door wondering whether or not her father would answer.

'Shall we pull over for a minute?' Carol suggested, she had taken one look at Prue and seen the turmoil inside of her head.

'Yes please.' Prue pulled the car over to the side of the road and turned it off before taking a couple of deep breaths to steady her nerves. She'd been through so much over the last couple of months what with her grandmother's death, the village hating her, her short-lived relationship with Elliot and now potentially meeting her father for the first time. She'd be lying to herself if she didn't admit that a big part of her was scared of rejection. After all, she'd been hated by the village and even Elliot had given up on her. Who knew whether her father would want anything to do with her?

'Prue, I may not have seen my nephew for a long time but I did know him very well. He was a kind and loving man and I honestly think he will be overjoyed to see you. I think he's probably been too scared to disrupt your life by contacting you. He's probably scared, too.' Carol leant across the car and took Prue's hand in hers. Prue hoped that the woman was right, at the very least she had to believe she was right. With one final deep breath Prue turned the key in the engine and began to press down on the accelerator.

'Come on, Carol.' She smiled at the old woman and they set off towards the house.

The SatNav directed them to a house that could only be described as average. There was nothing that made it special. It was a red brick, mid-terrace house with a brown door. Prue was a little disappointed that the house didn't give anything away about her father's personality or his life. Or perhaps it did, perhaps his life was just average. Prue was well aware that her mind was running away with itself at this point and so she grabbed her handbag and made her way out of the car before she could think of anything else. Carol followed her and came round to her side of the road. Both women stood staring up at the house in front of them. The driveway in front of the house lay empty and Prue was worried that her father was out. It was a Monday after-all, there was a high possibility that he was out at work.

'Perhaps he doesn't have a car.' Carol must have been thinking the exact same as Prue.

'There's only one way to find out. Are you ready?' Carol nodded in agreement and the two women made their way up the driveway to the front door.

Without thinking about it Prue lifted her hand and knocked on the door. Time seemed to stop as they stood there waiting to see whether anyone would answer the door. Prue had to remind herself that even if someone did answer the door, it might not necessarily be her father. After all, she had already had one disappointment in finding him. After what seemed like hours, but was probably only 30 seconds, the door began to open and Prue felt her breath catch in her throat. Was she about to meet her father?

As the man on the other side of the door came into view Prue felt as though her whole world had been tipped on its side. There was no mistaking who it was on the other side of the door, it was her father. Prue had always known that she shared her looks with her mother, however looking at the man in front of her she could see that she had inherited both his jaw line and his lips. Prue found herself utterly speechless as she stared into her father's eyes. He seemed to be just as taken-back as she was as his mouth opened and closed but no words were coming out.

'Robert?' Carol's voice brought Prue back into the present and she shook her head to force herself to concentrate on the moment and begin to find her words again. Prue watched as he turned to look at the woman beside her and a look of recognition fell across this face, he hadn't even noticed she was there until she had spoken.

'Auntie Carol!' He exclaimed, he shook his head in disbelief. Prue thought about how much of a shock this must be for him. At least she had been able to process everything and begin to come to terms with meeting her father. Robert hadn't had any chance to prepare himself for this moment.

'Robert, I'd like you to meet your daughter, Prue.' Carol's smile grew even bigger as she revelled in the moment as Robert met his daughter for the first time.

'Hello.' Prue waved, feeling incredibly shy and not knowing what the etiquette was for meeting your long-lost father for the first time. Was she suppose to embrace him and immediately start calling him dad? Or should she call him Robert? She wished she had thought all of this through before she was stood on his doorstep face-to-face with him.

'Hello, Prue.' He smiled back at her, looking completely stunned. Thankfully he also looked as though he had no idea what the etiquette was. It was somewhat comforting to know that neither of them knew how to act in the situation.

'Can we come in or would you prefer we popped out for a coffee?' Thankfully they both had Carol there to prompt them.

'Please, come in.' Robert stood aside to allow them both into the house. Prue couldn't help but observe the fact that the hallway was just as bland as the outside of the house had been. White walls, beige carpet and not one single picture lined the walls. There was something quite sad about just how bare this little space was.

'The living room is the first door on the left. Would you excuse me for a moment, I better call work and tell them I won't be coming in until later.' Robert made his way further down the hallway as Prue and Carol let themselves into the living room to wait for him.

The room had the same white walls and beige carpet, however there was one splash of colour that stood out in the uninspiring room. Above the fireplace hung a large picture of a man and a woman dressed in bright colours. As they waited for Robert to return Prue made her way over to the picture to take a closer look. Prue was surprised to see that the picture was of her mother and Robert. They were stood in front of the door to the bookshop both with huge smiles on their faces and pure happiness sparkling in their eyes. It was the kind of photo that made you smile just looking at it.

'That's my favourite picture of Dottie.' Robert walked back into the room and came to stand beside Prue as they both stared up at the picture. Prue had known that her mother was Dorothy to most people but to her closest friends and family she had always been Dottie. There was a tendency in her family to adopt a shortened version of your name.

'She looks very happy.' Prue replied politely, a little part of her was jealous that the man stood next to her had known her mother. Prue's mother had died when she was so young she didn't have any proper memories of her. She only had those fake memories, which originate from a photo or a video clip and over time you convince yourself that you remembered being there.

'She was.' Robert gave a wistful sigh as he turned away from the picture and went to sit on the arm chair that was tucked away in the bay window. Even the sofas were a shade of taupe. Prue was now sure she didn't get her artistic flare and love for history from her father. Perhaps it was a trait that she had unknowingly inherited from her grandmother.

As a silence fell upon the room Prue decided to go and sit next to Carol on the sofa. She hoped that someone would encourage the conversation as for the first time in her life Prue was utterly speechless.

'I have to be honest Prue, I don't really know what to say. Don't get me wrong, I'm over the moon to see you and I've dreamed about this day for so many years. I just don't know what to say.' Prue could safely say that she had inherited her awkwardness from her father.

'I'm not too sure where to start either.' Prue replied with a nervous laugh, how were they ever going to forge a relationship when they were both just sat there enjoying the silence?

'Like father, like daughter.' Carol commented, making them all laugh.

'What brings you here, Prue? I mean, why now?' Prue was grateful for a conversation starter, she only wished it could have been a question that was easier to answer.

'My grandmother died recently and so I've gone home, to Ivy Hatch. Whilst I've been sorting everything out I discovered that the bookshop existed and from there I began to learn about your relationship with my mother. If I'm completely honest I hadn't given much thought to having a father before that. Obviously I'd wondered what you were like but I'd kind of resigned myself to never knowing.' Prue felt self-conscious as she finished her little speech. This was the first time her father was meeting her, which meant that everything she said and did would form his opinion on her. She only hoped he would be proud of her.

Robert asked a few more questions about Prue's life and how she had come back to the village. In turn, Prue asked her own questions and she learned that her father was a carpenter, he had his own little workshop nearby and was also contracted out by local builders. There was nobody special in his life, there never had been since her mother. A part of Prue felt very sad to know that he had completely given his heart to her mother and had never been able to move on. He must have lived a very quiet life, no wonder his house was so beige.

'What happened to the bookshop?' Robert asked, his eyes suddenly sparkled with intrigue.

'I've just recently re-opened it.'

'I met your mother in that bookshop. She always said our eyes met over the top of a romance novel, although that's not strictly true.' Tears formed in Robert's eyes as he indulged himself in his own memories. It wasn't something he often allowed himself to do but today was an exception.

'How did you meet then?' Prue asked, although she had read about it in her mother's diary she wanted to hear the same story from her father's point of view. Today wasn't just about meeting her father, it was a chance to find answers to all the unanswered questions that she had swimming around her head.

'That's a story for another day.' A funny look crossed Robert's face, he wasn't quite ready to share that story with Prue yet. It was a memory that he cherished dearly and it felt like the only part of Dottie that he had left. For Prue his words made her smile, he was already thinking about the next time they met. In all their awkward-glory they were still making some progress and slowly getting to know each other.

'We ought to be making a move.' Prue commented. They had been there for a few hours and in all honesty she felt exhausted from the roller coaster of emotions and the effort of trying to open up to a complete stranger. Today was just the start of their newfound-relationship, they didn't have to learn everything about one-another in one sitting.

'Of course, you have a long drive home.' Robert stood up ready to see them to the door. Prue felt a small pang in her heart at the idea of leaving but she knew it was for the best. She needed some time alone to process everything that had happened. Once she had done that she could consider how they moved their relationship on to become more familiar.

They said their goodbyes and Robert even leant forward to give Prue a brief but awkward hug.

'Why don't you come down for tea on Sunday? I know Prue will be working in the shop but we could pop in and see her and once it's shut we can all have dinner together?' Prue could have kissed Carol for her genius plan. It would give them both a week to come to terms with everything but it meant that they had their next visit planned. It also meant that Prue would be on home turf, which would hopefully ease some of the awkwardness.

'That sounds brilliant, good-bye!' Robert stood at the door, waving them off until they had turned out of the road and were no longer in eye sight.

CHAPTER TWENTY EIGHT

Prue wasn't quite sure how she drove home, it was all a bit of a blur. Herself and Carol were silent for the majority of the drive home, both of them were reflecting on the day's events. Prue was conscious that Carol hadn't got much of a chance to speak to Robert, however she knew that Carol had done that on purpose to allow her some time to speak to her father.

'How are you feeling?' Carol asked as they drove over the rickety bridge, which signalled they were only twenty minutes away from the village.

'If I'm honest I'm just feeling confused. I suppose I had this idea that I'd see my father and we'd instantly click. I was silly, I know but it doesn't make it any easier.' Prue felt tears prickle in her eyes as she voiced her thoughts out loud. She had to concentrate hard on the road in front of her, now was not the time to succumb to her emotions.

'It was never going to be like it is in films Prue. I think you both did really well. You've met each other and got that awkward first meeting out of the way with. I'm proud of you, Prue.' The sincerity in Carol's voice didn't help Prue's attempts to fight the tears. She was right though, the first meeting was out the way with, now they had to concentrate on building a relationship together. There was also the prospect of hearing all the memories that her father had to share. Prue's love for the past was rearing its ugly head again and she couldn't shake Elliot's words.

Perhaps it was time she tried living in the present a little more.

Prue dropped Carol off at her cottage and declined her invitation to have dinner with her. It had been such a long day that Prue just wanted to go home and relax. She also really wanted a large gin fizz. As Prue drove up the driveway to the manor she felt a familiar uneasiness, although she was sure Arnold would not subject her to anymore harassment she still worried every time she went home. She just had to hope that she hadn't upset anyone else in the village.

Once inside Prue poured herself a large gin and went in search of her laptop, where she had last left it in the library. She had got a little carried away the other morning when she discovered an online book auction. Needless to say the bookshop wouldn't need restocking for approximately another five years. It was an investment in the bookshop's future, at least that was what she was telling herself.

With her laptop in hand Prue decided to sit in the living room for a change, usually she avoided it as it felt so empty without her grandmother sat in her armchair. Prue had to stop living in the shadow of the manor's memories and previous inhabitants, it was her home now. With a newfound confidence Prue walked into the living room and looked around, where should this new (and possibly improved) Prue sit? Despite her decision to live in the present Prue couldn't bring herself to sit in her grandmother's armchair and so she made her way over to one of the three sofas, each one was a plum colour. They had been Prue's choice when her grandmother decided the room needed a facelift and had sought Prue's help in ordering furniture online. The room boasted beautifully restored original floorboards, with cream walls and lots of handpicked artwork. Prue remembered traipsing around Brighton on one of her grandmother's rare visits as they looked around all the antique shops for pictures. On the back wall hung Prue's favourite painting, it was of a victorian child with ringlets, an angelic smile and a little teddy bear in her hand. It had pulled on Prue's heartstrings as she thought about how the girl's picture had just been discarded. A person that had been forgotten about. Prue couldn't bear the thought and so, to her grandmother's despair, she bought the painting.

Prue didn't want to dwell on her memories of how the living room came to be decorated this way, after all she was suppose to be living in the present. The sofa wasn't the most comfortable but it would do for now and so Prue took her seat and opened up her laptop. Once the machine had started up she went in search of some clothing websites. If she was going to stop living in the past then the first thing she needed to do was update her wardrobe. To say Prue had never ordered any clothes online would be a lie - there had been that one time she had to order a white vest top for a halloween party. After a shameful amount of time she finally stumbled across a couple of sites that looked promising.

Seeing her father today had made Prue realise just how harmful living in the past can be. He had never moved on from her mother and so his life was empty. Both his empty house and vacant eyes had made it clear that he had stopped living his life after losing Dorothy Clemonte. Robert was now living each day in his memories, reliving each one over and over to convince himself that he was happy. Prue had realised that she didn't want to follow in his footsteps. She had a life to live and she wanted to live it. Her clothes would be the first step to her living in the moment.

Two hours later Prue had just finished her fourth gin fizz and was about to input her payment details for her new wardrobe. It had been rather stressful trying to decide what clothes to buy. In the space of a few minutes she had to decide what her new style was going to be. Eventually, she opted to keep it simple with lots of jeans and plain t-shirts, at least she thought that was what she had settled on. Perhaps gin cocktails and online shopping were not the most sensible combination. After a few wrong attempts Prue finally entered her bank details and clicked on the next day delivery. She took a deep breath before she clicked the confirm button and paid the online retailer a small fortune.

Perhaps this was what a quarter life crisis looked like.

CHAPTER TWENTY NINE

The following day Prue woke up with a pounding headache, perhaps she should have stopped after her fourth gin. Instead she had continued drinking until she fell into bed in the early hours of the morning. She had convinced herself that she deserved a few gins after having met her father for the first time. However, if she had been completely honest with herself the reason she kept topping up her glass was not because of her father, it was because of Elliot. She was still trying to numb the heartbreak. His words were still bouncing around her head and so Prue had used alcohol to silence them. It had worked to an extent, until she had decided to text him telling him that she hoped he went bald early. In hindsight, it probably wasn't the most mature way to handle the situation but it had made her giggle as she felt a sense of satisfaction as she hit the send button. In the harsh light of the day she realised just how childish that text had been and wishing someone went bald wasn't exactly the best comeback imaginable.

Prue groaned and lifted her head from the pillow, there was no point wallowing all day, she had to get out of bed and face the day. It was the only day this week for her to get anything done, she would be at the bookshop after today. The novelty of running a bookshop was starting to wear off and Prue was yearning to find some valuation work, she missed the opportunity to look at an item and ponder over its history. Although perhaps running a bookshop was more suited to the present day Prue -

the girl who had promised herself she would stop living in the past. With a sigh Prue dragged herself out of bed and went in search of some painkillers, there had to be something in this house that would stop the pounding in her head.

After a few minutes searching Prue found some paracetamol in one of the kitchen drawers and she quickly took them followed by a glass of water. As she was stood contemplating whether or not she could stomach any breakfast there was a knock at the front door. Thankfully a couple of days ago the broken door had been replaced and standing in its place was a contraption that made Fort Knox look easy to break into. The last thing Prue wanted was to see anyone but she couldn't just leave whoever it was standing on the doorstep and so she tightened her dressing gown belt and went to see who it was.

With a sickening realisation Prue saw a delivery driver stood on the driveway surrounded by boxes. She had forgotten that she had spent a small fortune (actually, there was nothing small about it) on clothes last night. With some reluctance she opened the door and signed on the dotted line. The man offered to bring the packages inside for her but Prue declined, she just wanted this over with as quick as possible. There was no way Prue could carry all these boxes upstairs, especially not in her hungover state, and so she dragged them all into the hallway and just stood and stared at them. She definitely needed a coffee before she could tackle this. A very strong, black coffee.

Once Prue had drunk half of her coffee she finally decided to face the chaos in her hallway and began to undo one of the boxes. If she was completely honest with herself the events of last night had become rather blurry and so she couldn't quite remember what she had ordered. With a growing sense of excitement Prue pulled out the first garment. A crop top. What had she been thinking? As Prue pulled more items out she noticed a few that she liked the look of and so she put them to one side, the rest she could return. She would have donated some of the items to a charity shop but she couldn't see the women of Ivy Hatch wearing a spangly diamanté handkerchief top.

Eventually, Prue had salvaged enough items to create a capsule wardrobe for herself and the other items were back in their boxes ready to be returned. At least it gave Prue the excuse to get ready and get out the house. With a final glance at the mountain of clothes Prue went off to shower and get ready for the day, even if it was nearly lunch time.

Once she had showered Prue put a small amount of make-up on, just to hide her hungover look. Instead of her signature curls she straightened her hair and pulled on a pair of jeans, a plain white t-shirt and a lightweight grey blazer. As Prue looked in the mirror she could barely recognise herself and yet she liked her reflection. It was a Prue that she hadn't see for many years and yet there was something about her appearance that made her happy. She was being herself today, no more hiding behind the past. It was a little scary but after everything Prue had been through over the last couple of months she knew she would be okay.

Somehow, Prue got all of the boxes inside her old Mini and she made her way into the village to drop them off at the post office. She couldn't wait to see everyone's face as she unloaded eight boxes.

'Can I help you?' Prue turned round to see Maggie standing behind her, a big smile on her face with her arms out to take the box from her.

'Thank you so much, Maggie.' Prue was really grateful for the help.

'Why are you sending so many boxes?' Maggie asked as she followed Prue into the Post Office with the last box.

'A deadly combination of alcohol, a pity party and a spot of retail therapy.' Maggie nodded in understanding, however Prue suspected she was not one who often indulged in much retail therapy.

'Do you have time for a coffee?' Other than getting some food shopping Prue had no other plans for the day and so she agreed to grab a coffee with Maggie.

The two women made their way to the cafe and Prue ordered them both a coffee and a couple of slices of cake. Her appetite was finally starting to come back after having only had coffee for breakfast.

'You look different, Prue.' Maggie suddenly looked very serious as they sat across the table from one another. All morning people had been giving Prue odd looks. It had been a long time since they had last seen her dressed in jeans and with straight hair.

'I realised I needed a change.' Prue shrugged her shoulders and looked towards the counter where their coffees were being prepared. She thought it might not be a good idea to tell Maggie about her argument with Elliot and how that had influenced her sudden change in appearance.

'Don't change too much Prue, you're perfect just the way you are.'

Prue sat in a stunned silence for a few minutes after Maggie had said that, she hadn't been expecting such kindness, especially from an almost stranger.

'I met my father yesterday.' Prue hadn't exactly been planning on telling Maggie, she'd been considering it and then all of a sudden her mouth blurted it out. Maggie was visibly surprised at Prue's revelation, she took a bite of her cake as she decided how to respond.

'Would you like to talk about it?' Maggie's face was full of sincere concern and as Prue thought about her question she realised that she was probably the only person in the village who would be genuinely happy to sit and listen to Prue.

'It didn't quite go how I expected, if I'm honest. I thought we'd click as soon as we met and we'd exchange stories about our life and it would immediately feel like the missing piece in my life had been filled.' Prue stirred her coffee as she tried not to let the tears fall from her eyes.

'It wasn't like that then?' Maggie asked, the concern in her tone was obvious.

'No. I mean, it wasn't awful. It was just awkward.'

'It was a long time ago so my memories are a little sparse but from what I do remember your father was like that even when he was with your mother. She found his awkwardness endearing. I remember one day she told me she liked him because he was her antithesis. She was the creative larger than life personality, meanwhile your father was shy and practical. They were chalk and cheese and yet they were perfect for each other.' Prue felt a smile spread across her face as she thought about how happy her mother must have been.

'I think that's the problem Maggie, I don't think we have anything in common. Actually, I do think we have one thing in common. We're both stuck living in the past and finding happiness in our memories, rather than creating new ones. '

'Prue, you've only met him once. Don't go jumping to conclusions. You've both been through a lot. It'll take time for you to open up to each other. As for you living in the past, I don't think you are Prue. I think perhaps you might have lost your way a little but you're finding yourself, anyone can see that. Just keep going Prue, look how far you've already come.'

Prue blinked in an attempt to clear the tears that had formed in her eyes. Somehow Maggie always seemed to know what the right thing to say was.

'Prue, I have to go, I've got a hair appointment in five minutes. Take care and you can always drop by for a chat. I know Arnold isn't the friendliest but you're always welcome at the farm.'

Prue gave Maggie a hug goodbye and then she sunk back down in her seat to finish her coffee and to go over their conversation in her head. Maggie was right, she had judged Robert already and she had only met him once. She had surprised him on his doorstep and then she was offended when he was awkward. In her short time back in the village Prue already felt like a new person and not just because she was now dressing differently. She had learnt to be patient and to appreciate everyone. There would be time for her and her father to bond in the future but for now they just had to get to know each other and feel comfortable in each other's company. Prue also needed to get to know herself again.

CHAPTER THIRTY

Prue was almost grateful for Wednesday to roll around, at least she could ensconce herself in the bookshop and sit back as the day trundled past. She was both excited and nervous for Sunday and so she intended to savour every moment of the next few days before her emotions went into overload and the panic set in. Prue had spoken to Katie last night and her friend had told her to stop being so silly and to stop stressing over Robert's visit at the weekend. What Katie didn't realise was that Prue couldn't stop stressing, there was an overwhelming amount of pressure around Robert's next visit. Realistically, Prue knew that not all parents and children got along, however the bond between family members kept them connected. In her situation there was no bond, if they didn't get along then there was nothing to cling on to, they could simply walk away from each other and continue with their lives. Prue couldn't let that happen though, not after coming so close to having a father in her life.

With a frustrated sigh Prue shook her head free of all her thoughts. She couldn't spend the next few days thinking like this, she would drive herself crazy. Instead she refocused her attention on her new capsule wardrobe - what did she want to wear for a day at work? Prue knew exactly what she wanted to wear; a navy tea dress that had been made from another of her mother's old garments. That wasn't looking towards the future though and so Prue opted for some white jeans and a cream cashmere jumper. She felt very out of her comfort zone but that was good, wasn't it? The whole point of this change in appearance was to ultimately change her outlook on life.

The day was slow with a handful of people popping in to buy books. Prue was starting to recognise some regular customers and so noticed a few that came in, browsed the shelves and left empty handed. Perhaps she should start up a library of some sorts but with a small subscription fee. As lunchtime approached Prue noticed a lull in customers as everyone went in search of some food, she herself was beginning to feel rather peckish. There was very little in the fridge and so Prue decided to treat herself to a sandwich from the cafe, she justified it by telling herself that she was supporting local businesses. In reality, she just really wanted one of their cheese and chutney doorstops.

As Prue ambled down the street towards the cafe she realised she was starting to feel more content with life. Slowly things were slotting into place. If she looked at where she was when she first moved to the village then it was clear she had made progress, she had also grown as a person. Now she just had to strive towards happiness. She had to concentrate on being herself and she hoped that building a relationship with her father would contribute towards that.

'Prue?' As someone called her name from behind Prue immediately felt her contentment ebb away as she recognised the voice. Reluctantly she turned around to come face-to-face with Elliot.

'I thought it was you. You look... different.' Prue wasn't sure whether to be offended by Elliot's remark or to just ignore it and so she chose the less stressful option and ignored it.

'What do you want Elliot?' Prue sighed, all she wanted was a yummy sandwich and to steal half an hour with a book before she opened the shop up again.

'I just wanted to see how you were doing.' He shrugged, refusing to make eye contact with her. Prue wondered if he felt guilty for moving on so quickly, or perhaps he felt guilty about what he had said to her last time they had spoken.

'I'm fine.' Prue's answer was short and she ensured her disdain towards him was obvious in the snappy tone that she used. Perhaps he would get the hint and leave her alone.

'I heard you found your father.' It wasn't a question, it was a statement and an opportunity for Prue to speak. However, she had no intention of speaking to Elliot about any of this, he would only use it in an argument against her in the future.

'I did. Now if you don't mind I'm going to leave. I'd like to eat something during my lunch break.' Without even saying a proper goodbye Prue turned and started walking towards the cafe, it took every ounce of self-control to stop herself from breaking into a run. She wanted to be as far away from Elliot Harrington as she possibly could be. After all that he had done and said to her how could he possibly stand there trying to encourage her to speak to him? He was as mad as his father.

After her encounter with Elliot the contentment that Prue had been feeling had completely left her. Prue got herself a sandwich from the cafe and took it back to the shop, however even food couldn't improve her mood. The afternoon dragged by slowly as she kept replaying her conversation with Elliot, over and over. Every now and then her mind would wander to how beautiful his eyes were or the memory of his hand in hers. She would then shake her head to rid herself of the memories and a sense of anger would come over her. Elliot Harrington had proven himself to be a disloyal and downright rude person, she had to stop thinking about him and make the effort to avoid him in the street.

That afternoon, Prue's sense of determination grew even more, she would be happy. It might take time and a lot of effort but she would find her happiness again and enjoy life. Never again would she allow another person to influence her life or her mood.

CHAPTER THIRTY ONE

The week went by surprisingly quickly, perhaps because Prue was somewhat dreading Sunday. Her determination to be happy relied on her forging a relationship with her father and so Sunday's meeting would be pivotal. As she locked up the shop on Saturday evening the sun was high in the sky but she knew she had another hour or two until it set. Prue set off towards the village shop and purchased a bunch of peonies, her grandmother's favourite flower. With the bunch of flowers in hand she jumped in her Mini and drove towards the cemetery. Her family were not buried at the village church, instead the Clemontes had a small mausoleum in the local cemetery, which had been there since before the church had been built.

As Prue stepped out of the car at the cemetery she felt a calmness wash over her. Some people were afraid of cemeteries, however Prue found them peaceful places to visit. Perhaps it was because she had been coming for so many years, her grandmother was adamant that they made a weekly visit to her mother's grave. Prue knew that even after she had left to go to university her grandmother had kept up that weekly ritual. A sense of guilt flooded Prue, she had neglected her mother and her grandmother with everything that was going on in her life. As Prue picked-up the bunch of flowers from the passenger seat she promised herself that she would come and visit more often.

Without even needing to think about where she was going Prue walked over towards the back of the cemetery where her family's mausoleum stood. There must have been almost fifty Clemontes buried here. Prue laid her flowers at the entrance and sat down on one of the steps. For the first time since her grandmother's death a sadness fell over her. She remembered coming here with her grandmother, they would both sit on the steps with a flask of tea and they would tell her mother about their week. It was a rare glimpse into Elizabeth Clemonte's heart and it was a moment that Prue would treasure forever. She hoped that her mother and grandmother were sat together now, drinking tea from a flask and watching over Prue as she sat there trying to find the right words to say.

'I miss you both.' Prue hadn't meant for the words to slip out but they did. It wasn't until that moment that she realised just how much she missed her family, particularly her grandmother. She hadn't been the kind of grandmother to give her endless cuddles and treat her to cinema trips and bags of sweets but she had been there for Prue. There was a hole in her life that would never be able to be filled by anyone else. Despite the sadness Prue was happy and felt lucky to have so many memories to look back on. For the first time in a while Prue felt content with her memories, she didn't want to focus on them but she was happy she had them to eventually look back on.

'I'd love to know what you would both tell me to do with my life right now.' Prue let out a wistful sigh as she tried to imagine what her family would say.

'Gran, you'd tell me to stop being so emotional and to show everyone who is in charge. I'm not very good at doing that though, you taught me everything you could but I'm just too much like mum.' Prue had heard endless stories about how her mother had always followed her heart, rather than her head. Prue had inherited her mother's passion for life alongside her grandmother's headstrong attitude. It made her determined to live her life and seek happiness. However, that was proving to be rather difficult right now, not that Prue was about to give in.

'What would mum say? I think she'd try and put a romantic

spin on everything. She'd tell me to mend bridges between myself and Elliot, to welcome my father into my life and to put my heart and soul into her bookshop.' Yes, that was what Dorothy Clemonte would have said and Elizabeth would have rolled her eyes at her daughter and yet a small part of her would have yearned to have the same outlook on life.

What would Prue do though? That was one question that Prue really didn't know the answer to. She had spent so long in the shadow of her grandmother's strong personality and the memories of her mother that she had forgotten to find herself. Begrudgingly she had to admit that Elliot did have a point, she needed to look towards the future. She had to grow into her own shoes and be the controlling force behind her life. Nobody else would do it for her and nobody else could make her happy. The burden lay firmly at Prue's feet and it was only now that she realised how much work she had to put into herself to truly be happy.

Sat here in the silence of the cemetery Prue felt at peace. There were two things that made her truly happy; being at work in an auction house and her time spent with Elliot. Unfortunately, spending time with Elliot was not an option, however she could begin to try and forge a career for herself here. Prue loved the bookshop but it was her mother's, not hers. The first step to being happy in her own skin was to do what made her happy and to forge her own future, starting with continuing her career.

CHAPTER THIRTY TWO

Sunday morning Prue woke with a new outlook on life. Her visit to the cemetery the previous evening had made her realise a few things. Prue did know a little about who she was, she enjoyed 40's fashion and she loved working in auction houses. It wasn't much but it was a start. With that in mind Prue dove back into her old wardrobe and threw on the navy tea dress that she had been dying to wear a few days ago. On Monday she would begin the search for some help in the bookshop so that she could go back to her own career. *The Vintage Bookshop of Memories* was her mother's project and Prue was incredibly happy to have it back up and running for everyone to enjoy. However, the bookshop held too many memories and Prue knew that if she stayed working there then her life wouldn't move on, she would still be living in the shadow of her mother's memory.

Prue Clemonte had to stop living in the past, she had to start living her life in the present. Starting with her father coming today; she wouldn't think about their last meeting and she wouldn't jump ahead to thinking about the kind of relationship she wanted to create. Prue was going to live in the moment and see what the day brought. She had planned ahead (that kind-of counted as living in the moment, right?) and had decided to bring a selection of books to dinner. She wanted to see whether reading was her father's achilles heel.

Every time someone stepped foot into the bookshop Prue's heart hammered in her chest but each time she was disappointed to see it wasn't Robert. As the hours ticked by Prue began to give up any hope of them actually popping in, perhaps something had happened and her father had been forced to cancel. In an attempt to distract herself Prue went into the little kitchenette whilst the shop was quiet to make herself a coffee.

'This place looks just how I expected it to!' Prue heard her father's voice from the shop floor, she was so excited she managed to slosh milk all over the counter. That didn't matter though, all that mattered was that he was here.

'Do you like it?' Prue asked, holding her breath. She hadn't realised just how important his reaction was to her. The bookshop had been a little bubble for her parents to be together and so she wanted to ensure she had done their memory justice.

'Prue, it's amazing. You've put your own stamp on it whilst still preserving everything. Did you know I made the balcony and the ladder? That was how your mother and I met.' This was the most animated that Prue had seen him and she could see Carol stood behind him with a huge smile on her face.

'I did know that. Can I get you both a drink?' Both declined and so Prue nipped back into the kitchenette to pick up her coffee and to wipe up the milk that had been spilt. Prue wondered whether she should tell Robert about her mother's diary. However, deep down she knew she wasn't ready to part with it yet and so she decided to keep it a secret for now, after all it was the only insight she had into her mother's mind.

When she walked back into the bookshop Carol was sat in the old chair flicking through one of the romance novels that Prue had just put out on the shelf. Meanwhile, her father was stood talking to Maggie and to Prue's shock stood next to Maggie was the blonde woman that she had seen Elliot with in the pub.

'Prue, I just popped in to ask you something when I bumped into your father. It's been years since I last saw him.' Maggie smiled warmly at Prue as she walked over to the little gathering. Prue felt a little awkward as she came to a stop next to her father as everyone's eyes were on her, including the mystery woman who had the cheek to be smiling at her. Prue dug her nails into the palms of her hands to stop herself from calling the woman some rather unpleasant names.

'Robert's come down to have dinner with myself and Carol this afternoon.' Prue explained, she felt the need to explain his sudden presence back in the village. There were bound to be some people who wouldn't be happy to see him back.

'That sounds lovely. I won't keep you long, I heard from Mrs Patterson that you're looking for someone to work in the shop and I'd like to put my name forward. I don't have much experience but I do love a good book.' Prue was slightly taken back, Maggie had been the last person she had expected to apply for the role and yet she couldn't think of anyone better suited. Her bubbly personality and love for reading was just what this little bookshop needed.

'That sounds perfect Maggie. Why don't we meet for lunch on Monday, my treat, and we can discuss it in a little more detail?'

'Yes, I'd like that very much, thank you Prue. Oh, how rude of me. Prue, this is Charlotte, my niece. She's studying law at university and so has been staying with us for a bit to do some work experience with Elliot.' Prue's mouth opened and closed but no words would come out. She was Maggie's niece, not Elliot's new girlfriend.

'Anyway Maggie, it was lovely to see you again.' Robert had noticed that his daughter was struggling to find the words to say and so he jumped in to save her. Prue couldn't have been more grateful if she had tried. Perhaps there was such a thing as an instant father-daughter bond.

'Bye, Maggie!' Prue managed to splutter out just as the two

women had walked out of the shop. She had judged Elliot and been so upset that he had moved on already and yet there he was trying to do a good deed and help a family member's career. However, that didn't change what he had said during their argument, his words had hurt her. They had made her come to some revelation though and helped her move forward with her life but he didn't need to know that.

'Are you okay?' Robert asked, his eyes searching Prue's face for some sign as to what was going on.

'She's head over heels in love with Maggie's son but the pair of them are too pig-headed to admit they want to be together.' Carol called from the comfort of her chair.

'There's a bit more to it than that.' Prue sighed and went to put her cup down on the counter, the last thing she needed was to spill it with all these books around her.

'Why don't you tell me while there's nobody else in the shop?'

Prue thought about it for a moment, perhaps it would be nice to hear someone else's opinion. After all, surely Robert would have her best interests at heart and so he would be one of the best people to confide in. Prue took a deep breath before telling Robert the whole story, including the argument that herself and Elliot had when he told her to stop living in the past.

'I think Carol is right, you are head-over-heels in love with him.' That wasn't really the reaction that Prue had been hoping for from her father. Why wasn't he offering to go round and tell him not to mess with his daughter? That was what fathers were suppose to do, right?

'Not anymore.' Prue huffed, breaking eye contact and staring down at the cold cup of coffee in front of her. Robert seemed ridiculously perceptive today.

'Prue, I'm not saying Elliot was right in what he said to you but

I think his heart was in the right place. I think deep down he thought that what he was saying to you was what you needed to hear. Perhaps he was right? Prue, don't make the same mistake that I have. I was never able to move on from your mother and I've not lived at all, I've just been re-living my memories. Be brave and go and live your life. '

God, parents could be so annoying sometimes. Even after a lifetime apart Robert could hit the nail on the head and preach parental advice as if he had been doing it her entire life.

'Okay, perhaps Elliot was right but that doesn't mean I should just go and forgive him.' Prue conceded.

'That's exactly what it means, you need to make things right with him.' Carol called over from her chair, she'd stayed quiet up until now.

'It's not just us though, is it Carol. Arnold hasn't exactly been helpful towards us getting to know each other.'

'You leave Arnold to me. He and I go back a long way.' Robert looked confident that he could change the man's opinion and Prue didn't have the energy left to argue. Prue glanced at the clock behind her, she only had fifteen minutes until closing time.

Robert and Carol waited with Prue until she had closed up and the three of them made their way back to Carol's for dinner, Prue with a large pile of books in her tote bag. Prue was trying not to think too much about the evening, she didn't need to add any additional pressure to the situation. She couldn't force a relationship or a bond between herself and Robert and so she just had to sit back and see what happened. It was incredibly scary to have no control over your own life but in that moment Prue knew that she just had to accept it and see what happened.

As Carol let them into her cottage the smell of dinner hit them, she had left a casserole in the oven.

'Carol, that smells amazing! Casserole is my favourite dinner.' Prue inhaled the smell again and felt her stomach rumble, lunch seemed so long ago.

'It's my favourite too.' Robert had a smile on his face as he made the confession. Finally, Prue had found something that they both had in common, of course it would be food related.

Carol instructed them both to take a seat at the table while she dished up, they both offered to help her but she wouldn't let them. Prue took her bag of books to the table with her and unpacked them onto the oak top.

'If you had to pick one of these, which one would you pick?' To some people this might be a strange way of judging someone's character but to a reader someone's book choice can reveal a lot about who they are.

Prue watched Robert as he took in the cover of each book and then turned each one over to read the blurb. He wasn't making any snap decisions based on the image on the front of the book, nor did he seem particularly drawn to a specific genre. Instead he was concentrating on the story and the content of the book. It was refreshing to see someone taking such care over what they read.

'This one.' Robert finally settled on one book. Prue was somewhat surprised to see that he had opted for the rom-com.

'Really?' Prue asked in shock. If she was honest with herself that was the book she would have picked.

'Yes. There's nothing better than a book with a big romance and a hint of comedy. It reminds you that there's still happiness and hope in the world.'

Prue thought about Robert's explanation for a moment and as she let his words sink in she realised that was just how she would justify picking the same book. Everyone needed a little more happiness in their life and for some people that kind of happiness could only be found in the form of a book.

As the night went on Prue found that Robert came out of his shell and they had a number of things in common, including their intense dislike for mushrooms. Carol kept apologising for putting mushrooms in the dinner but they had both laughed and told her it was fine. Not once did they talk about the past, they firmly kept the conversation in the present and their hopes for the future. Prue told Robert about how she wanted to pick-up her career again and he had encouraged her to follow her heart.

'I'm thinking about going back to Brighton for a few days to have a chat with some of my old contacts. I'm hoping they might be able to put me in touch with some people in the area.' Prue had been mulling this over in her head for some time now. Not only did she want to find some new contacts but she also yearned for the bright lights of a bustling city. She needed to go back and see the city again to make sure that staying in Ivy Hatch was right for her.

Everyone agreed that it sounded like a good idea and so Prue left that night with a huge smile on her face. She was slowly forging a relationship with her father and she also had plans to go back to her favourite city. Life was starting to look up, perhaps this whole living in the present wasn't such a bad thing.

CHAPTER THIRTY THREE

Monday morning came quickly, it felt as though Prue had only just laid her head on the pillow when the piercing sound of her alarm pulled her from her dreams. Despite the early wake-up call Prue couldn't be too upset as she was looking forward to her lunch with Maggie today. Before that though she had to be at the bookshop to accept another delivery of books. Prue's love for auctions and books was getting a little out of control. However, there was no time to lie in bed and ponder her life choices, Prue needed to be up and out of the house quickly.

Half an hour later Prue was yawning as she made herself a coffee in the kitchenette at the bookshop. There were some benefits to her new style and not having to curl her hair in the morning was one of them. Instead, she had platted her hair the previous evening and so she had glossy black waves today. She had teamed her new hair-do with a pair of blue skinny jeans and a denim shirt. A few days into her new look and she was already risking double denim, Prue barely recognised herself anymore. Especially when she walked past a mirror and saw a smile on her face. Life finally felt like it was back on track, or at the very least it was almost back on track.

The books were delivered and Prue spent the morning writing little notes to pop inside them. Despite her new outlook on life she still wanted to keep this little tradition and she felt that it gave the little bookshop a fun twist. Prue had even taken to writing short stories in some of the books. It kept her busy but she loved every second of it. Once the notes were written she had to find places for the books on the shelves, which were already straining under the weight of thousands of books. It truly was a treasure-trove of books.

'Prue?' Maggie's voice came from the other side of the shut door. Prue jumped down from the ladder and went to open the door, she glanced at her watch on the way and realised she was late for lunch.

'Maggie, I'm so sorry I didn't realise what the time was, I've been so busy unpacking all the new books I ordered.'

'Please, don't apologise Prue. I guessed where you would be. Would you like some help?' Prue glanced back at the pile of books on the floor, she would sort them out this afternoon.

'No, come on, let's go and have some lunch.'

The two women walked towards the cafe and Maggie asked Prue about her evening with her father. With a huge smile on her face Prue told Maggie about their dinner at Carol's and how much they had found they had in common.

'I'm so happy for you Prue. Your mum would be very proud of you.'

Prue felt tears form in her eyes at Maggie's words, she really hoped that her mother would be proud.

The two women entered the cafe and took the table by the window again, it was quickly becoming their 'usual' spot. Prue was absolutely starving after her busy morning and so she opted for a toasted cheese sandwich with a side salad, meanwhile Maggie ordered a jacket potato with cheese and beans. There was no smashed avocado on sourdough in Ivy Hatch.

'Thank you for being so kind to me, Maggie.' Prue couldn't help but feel incredibly lucky to have met someone like Maggie, an almost mother figure who was happy to listen to Prue's woes.

'I had a lot of respect for your mother Prue. She hated that her place in society was trying to dictate her life and so she fought against it in order to be happy. I think we should all do that. Nothing but our happiness should dictate what we do with our lives.'

'That's very true Maggie and that actually ties in to why I'm looking for some help in the bookshop.' Prue went on to explain her plans of getting back into her previous career.

'If that's what will make you happy Prue then you have to do it. I think it's brilliant that you've restored the bookshop and re-opened it. The bookshop is a lovely memorial for your mother but it's also beneficial for the village. You've done your bit for your family and the village, now you have to follow your own career path. That's where I come in, running the bookshop.'

The two women discussed the shop and agreed that Maggie would work four days a week and Prue would work Sunday until they could find someone else to cover. It was the perfect partnership as Maggie had been looking for something to do, outside the farm and the farm's kitchen.

'I know you think I'm doing you a favour Prue but honestly, this means so much to me. I've given my entire life to that farm and my family but now I want something for me.' There were unshed tears in Maggie's eyes as she made the admission.

'No tears. Here's to our new partnership.' Prue picked up her cup of tea and clicked mugs with Maggie as they both grinned at each other.

'Prue, I know you're not going to like what I have to say but I wouldn't be a very good mother if I didn't at least try. Will you speak to Elliot?' Prue had almost been expecting Maggie to bring it up at some point. After all, she was Elliot's mother and she wanted him to be happy.

'I'm not sure Maggie. I think too much might have happened between us. There's also the village to think about, I don't want history to repeat itself.'

'Prue, you've won everyone over I don't think they'd object to you dating Elliot. Most of the residents understand that times have changed and there are no longer such barriers in society.'

Prue didn't know what to say to Maggie. Should she tell her that their biggest hurdle was Arnold? Prue wondered just how much Maggie knew about her husband's bullish behaviour.

'Prue?' Maggie asked, in a tone that made Prue feel like a scolded child. Maggie knew there was something that Prue wasn't telling her and she intended to find out what it was.

'Maggie, I really don't want to be the person to tell you this.'

'Prue, please just tell me what is going on.'

Prue took a deep breath to collect her thoughts. She was sure Maggie would know if she lied or missed anything out, she had no choice, she had to tell her everything. With one final glance at the floor, hoping it would open up and swallow her whole, Prue began to tell Maggie what Arnold had done to try and get Prue out of the village and break her and Elliot up.

'I'm going to kill him.' The anger was apparent both on Maggie's face and in her tone, she was furious.

'Please Maggie, I don't want to cause anymore trouble.' Prue felt an unimaginable amount of guilt, she knew she had just stirred up a lot of trouble in the Harrington household.

'Cause trouble? Prue, the only person causing trouble around here is my husband. Let me get this right, you broke up with Elliot because Arnold told you to?'

Prue was left speechless for a moment as she considered the question. At the time she had convinced herself that she was ending things because she didn't want them to suffer the same fate as her parents. However, in retrospect Prue knew that she had ended things because she wanted a quiet life in the village and she just wanted to be happy. Now that her life was slowly coming together there was still a piece missing and she knew that however hard she searched for that missing piece, Elliot was the only one who would ever fill it.

'Yes.' Prue finally felt the courage to admit it out loud. She looked up to see Maggie's eyes reflecting her own sadness.
'I'm going to fix this Prue and rest assured that my husband will never interfere in your life ever again.' Maggie squeezed Prue's hand before almost running out of the cafe to find her husband.

Prue was left sat at the table feeling completely speechless. Had she really just admitted that she wouldn't have dumped Elliot if not for Arnold's interference? It was true though. The time they had spent together had been utterly perfect, he had made her smile when she hadn't thought it were possible. Prue didn't know what would happen next, all she knew was that something was about to happen. Maggie Harrington was the kind of woman that got things done and if she wanted Elliot and Prue back together then they would be.

CHAPTER THIRTY FOUR

After Prue's lunch with Maggie on Monday Prue couldn't stop thinking about how things in the Harrington household were. Maggie had come into work on Wednesday morning ready for Prue to show her the ropes, she didn't give anything away as to how her chat with Arnold had gone. Neither of them spoken about what had happened in the cafe and Maggie didn't volunteer any information. However, Maggie's red and puffy eyes told Prue that things at home were not good. On Thursday morning Maggie had arrived at work on time but with unshed tears filling her eyes.

'Oh Maggie, sit down. I'm going to make us both a cup of tea and you're going to talk to me.' Prue didn't give Maggie a chance to argue, instead she went straight to the kitchenette and put the kettle on. A few minutes later she walked back into the bookshop with two steaming mugs of tea and a packet of chocolate biscuits under her arm.

'What's happened?' Prue asked as she placed their cups of tea down and offered Maggie a biscuit.

'Nothing has happened Prue, that's the problem. I know Arnold's flaws, I always have but I also see the softer side to him. Over the years I hoped that I could bring out the softer side and his prejudices and archaic views on life would disappear. He promises me he'll change but nothing ever happens. We've been arguing constantly about the way he behaved towards you and

Elliot.' Maggie stopped to take a sip from her tea and to compose herself before she began crying.

'Maggie, please don't argue about me. Despite everything I can understand Arnold's dated views on life. I know that the village had hoped my mother would marry and secure the land.' Prue meant what she was saying, a part of her did understand the frustrations of the people. After a chat with Mr Adley, Prue had discovered that the failed arranged marriage had caused lots of problems and lots of villagers had lost land. Her grandmother had eventually bought the land back but the damage had already been done.

'We lost some of our farm when your mother declared her love for your father. The Devons reacted by taking back all the land that they were renting to us. Although we have since got it back, your grandmother made sure of that. It's just, Arnold never forgave your family for that, in his eyes your mother should have put the village first.' It was clear from Maggie's tone that she disagreed with her husband's opinion.

'I'm sorry for the trouble my mother caused but she had her own life to live.' Despite knowing that Maggie was on her side, Prue couldn't help but jump to her mother's defence.

'I understand that Prue and deep down Arnold does too. He's bitter because he never wanted to take over the farm, his father forced him to. Anyone who defies expectations and lives their own life angers him because he wasn't brave enough to do the same.' Maggie's tone was weary and Prue suspected that Arnold's attitude was something that caused a lot of aggravation in the Harrington household. It also explained why he was so annoyed at Elliot.

'Maggie, right now I'm not worried about Arnold, it's you I'm worried about. It's time for you to be happy and to live your life.' Prue felt for the tired looking woman sat opposite her, she had dedicated her life to her husband and her children, it was now time she followed her own heart.

'I'll be fine Prue but thank you for your concern.' Maggie had taken a deep breath and had composed herself.

'Maggie, a few of the cottages are going to be empty soon as the occupants have decided not to sign the new contracts. I'd like to offer you one of them, no rent and you can stay for as long as you want to.' Prue had been thinking this through for a few days now, she wanted Maggie to know that she had options, she didn't have to stay with Arnold because she had nowhere else to go.

'Thank you Prue, I really appreciate that.'

'Promise me you'll seriously consider it, Maggie. I want you to be happy. You were kind to both myself and my mother when everyone else hated us and I'd like to be able to return your kindness.' Prue had to take a deep breath as she found herself becoming emotional, she really did appreciate everything that Maggie had done for her.

'I promise.' Maggie smiled and stood up to take her empty cup into the kitchenette, signalling that the conversation was over.

Prue hoped that Maggie really did consider her offer. She wanted the woman to be happy and Prue couldn't imagine how anybody could be happy living with a man like Arnold Harrington.

CHAPTER THIRTY FIVE

As the week continued Maggie didn't mention her home life again and Prue didn't want to push her. Whilst worrying about Maggie, Prue was also on edge everyday wondering when she might hear from Elliot. She was yet to hear anything from him and she was beginning to give up hope. That was until Saturday morning, when Maggie was sat behind the till, whilst Prue rearranged the children's books. The bookshop's door swung open and in walked Elliot, looking as handsome as ever, with a huge smile across his face.

'Good morning!' He called out in a loud voice, thankfully there were no customers in the shop.

'Hello, Elliot.' Prue almost whispered as she dropped the books in her hands and turned to face him.

'I'm taking you away.' He announced, looking smug. Prue wasn't quite sure what to say in response, that had been the last thing she had expected him to say. Actually, she had been expecting him to start with an apology.

'Elliot darling, I know you're excited but perhaps be a little more coherent with your words.' Prue couldn't help but laugh at Maggie's chastisement and the look of adolescent sulkiness that flashed across Elliot's face.

'Why don't you go and make yourself a coffee, mum?' Elliot suggested, the sulky look was still plastered across his face. Maggie laughed and excused herself before shutting the kitchenette door behind her.

'Let's try that again, shall we?' Prue suggested. Her heart was thumping against her chest as she looked up into his eyes.

'I'm sorry for everything that's happened, Prue. You make me so happy and there's nothing I want more than to be with you. Mum told me everything, including your plans to go to Brighton. I want to go with you, let's have a weekend away, just the two of us. I think we need some time away from this village.'

'That sounds perfect.' Prue whispered, stepping closer so that she was in touching distance of Elliot. Some time alone without the entire village watching them was just what they needed.

'Good because I've already bought the train tickets for next weekend and booked us a hotel.' Elliot was almost glowing with happiness as he explained his plans to Prue. It was perfect.

Without any thought to customers walking in Prue stepped forward and reached up on her tip toes to give Elliot a kiss. It didn't last for long though, they were interrupted by someone clearing their throat behind them. Prue stepped back and put a hand to her cheek, it was scorching. She didn't even want to consider how red her cheeks were.

'I'm glad to see you two have made up.' Prue looked around Elliot to see her father stood in the doorway, she hadn't been expecting him to pop round today.

'Robert!' Prue exclaimed, she still wasn't ready to call him dad but he seemed to be okay with that, one day she would. 'I'd like you to meet Elliot. Elliot, I'd like you to meet Robert, my father.'

As introductions were made Maggie slipped back out from her hiding place and joined in the conversation. She professed her happiness for them and she promised Prue that the bookshop would be fine whilst she was in Brighton.

'Actually Prue, I didn't just drop by for a chat. I've heard that

Wisteria Cottage in the village might be coming up to rent?' Robert was right, the couple that lived there had decided not to renew their contract. It wasn't that they disliked Prue, it was just that they had decided to move closer to their daughter and son-in-law.

'Yes, that's true. Did you have someone in mind?' Prue was wondering who her father might be planning on recommending village life to.

'Well, if it's okay with you I was considering renting it myself. My work is flexible and so I see no reason as to why I can't move.' Prue was almost speechless, her father moving to the village? Was it possible to experience too much happiness on one day? If it was then Prue was definitely going into happiness overload.

'Of course you can. Are you sure you want to come back here?' Prue tried to reign in her growing excitement, she wanted to make sure that being here was what her father wanted, not just what he thought he should do.

'I want to come back Prue. You're here and it'll be nice to feel closer to your mother again. I'd also love to help out in the shop sometimes.' The smile on Robert's face was genuine and Prue couldn't help but return it.

'Then Wisteria Cottage is yours.' Prue could almost jump up and down with joy.

'Whilst we're having this happy little get together Prue, I was wondering if I could take you up on your offer?' Maggie's face was apprehensive, as though Prue might revoke her offer.

'Oh Maggie, nothing would make me happier.' Prue hugged the woman as both men looked on confused.

'What's going on mum?' Elliot asked as the two women finally pulled away from their embrace.

'I'm going to be Robert's new neighbour.' Maggie's excitement had dampened as she waited to see what her son's reaction would be to the news she was leaving his father.

'Oh mum, I'm so happy for you.' Now it was Elliot's turn to hug his mother.

'Are you sure?' Maggie asked, wiping the tears from her eyes.

'Mum, I've been trying to persuade you to leave that farm for years. You're not happy there and you deserve to be happy.'

Prue stood there taking in the sight in front of her. She had come home to the village with nobody, but here stood in her little shop, were the three people that meant the world to her. Everyone was finally finding some happiness in their lives and that alone made Prue's heart want to burst.

CHAPTER THIRTY SIX

The most important thing here was not to panic, Prue reminded herself. Packing for a weekend away was always going to be difficult, however for Prue it was made even more difficult by her opposing styles. Eventually, she settled on items from both sides of her wardrobe. The mixture seemed to feel more like her, rather than just sticking to one style. Just as Prue had managed to zip up her suitcase Elliot had pulled up outside the manor to drive them to the train station. The car journey itself wasn't too awkward, the worst part had been when Elliot went to greet Prue with a kiss and she had offered her cheek. They'd just ignored it though and climbed into the car. Prue hadn't seen much of Elliot as he had been busy at work so that he could take time off for their trip. They had met for a drink in the pub on Wednesday evening and it had been lovely, if not a little awkward. Prue was hoping that a long weekend together would help dispel any awkwardness and they could look towards their future.

Now, here they were sat on the train together hurtling towards Brighton and Prue could feel the excitement boiling up inside of her. The village would always be home but a change would be nice and a change with Elliot by her side would be even nicer. They were going to enjoy their weekend together and then on Monday Prue would go and visit some contacts, whilst Elliot met up with some old friends from university. Monday could wait though, Prue was looking forward to the weekend that they had together.

'Would you like a strawberry bonbon?' Elliot asked, producing a paper bag filled with the pink sugary delights. Prue took one and laughed to herself, no doubt the strawberry bonbons had been Maggie's idea.

'So where are we staying?' Prue asked, until then she hadn't given much thought to what hotel Elliot might have booked. She had been too busy overthinking spending the weekend with him.

'I've picked one on the seafront, it should also have a sea view.'

'Sounds perfect.' Prue sighed and relaxed into her seat as she chewed on her sweet. It felt like only yesterday she had packed up all of her belongings and got the train back to Ivy Hatch for her grandmother's funeral. A few months later here she was going back to Brighton with Elliot by her side. How life had changed. Katie had insisted that they meet for brunch on Sunday and Prue couldn't wait to catch up with her friend and finally introduce her to Elliot. It was about time Prue started merging her old life and her new life in order to find herself. Although Prue found it somewhat scary to not have a grasp on who she was, she also found it exciting. She had the opportunity to get to know herself and shape herself into whoever she wanted to be.

'Prue, I'm sorry for what I said about you living in the past. I love your appreciation of the past and I also love your fashion sense.' Prue could see Elliot taking in her outfit as he spoke. Today she had stepped out of her comfort zone with an above the knee red gingham short dress. It was flouncy and fun, just what Prue needed right now.

'Thank you for apologising. I'm not saying you were right to say what you did but it did make me think. I think you helped me to move my life in the right direction. I was living in the past, so much that I'd lost myself in it. You made me realise that I had to enjoy being me.' It was nice to finally clear the air between them. Elliot leant over and took Prue's hand in his and squeezed it.

'How's your mum?' Prue asked, she had been so busy packing for their weekend away that she hadn't had a chance to speak to Maggie.

'She's okay. As you can imagine my father didn't take the news well. She's moved in with me until the cottage becomes vacant.' The cottage would be empty in the next two weeks but Prue had been planning to renovate the place before Maggie moved in. Perhaps she could stay at Elliot's and Elliot could stay at the manor, depending on how the weekend went.

They spent the rest of the journey in a comfortable silence, watching as the world passed them by as they sat content in their own little bubble of happiness. As they exited the station at Brighton Elliot hailed them a taxi and gave the driver the name of the hotel they were staying at. Prue couldn't take her eyes off of the sparkling blue sea as they drove towards the hotel. When Elliot had said he had booked a hotel along the seafront Prue hadn't expected it to be quite so extravagant. The hotel was beautiful with floor-to-ceiling windows looking out towards the beach. The room itself was nautical themed with a huge driftwood bed in the centre of it, facing the window so that you could look out to sea whilst snuggled under the duvet. It was utter perfection.

'This is amazing!' Prue exclaimed as she stood by the window looking out towards the sea.

'It is isn't it.' Elliot agreed as he walked over to her and wrapped his arms around her.

'Thank you for this.' Prue turned around in his arms so that she was facing him.

'I love you Prue.' Elliot almost whispered it, there was a look of hesitation in his eyes as to whether or not now was the right moment to confess his feelings.

'I love you Elliot.' Prue replied, she reached up on her tip toes and kissed him.

After a late lunch from the room service menu they decided to go for a little wander along the seafront and wind their way through the Lanes. It was romantic as they strolled hand in hand through the throngs of people and yet nobody recognised them. They appreciated every second of being able to be together in public without anyone knowing anything about them or having an opinion on their relationship. It was so refreshing to experience and it allowed them to pick their relationship back up and become stronger. When they returned to the village they would be ready to face everyone and their opinions. For now though, they were happy being lost amongst the crowds.

EPILOGUE

Someone coughed from behind, making Prue jump and drop her clipboard, with a frustrated sigh she turned around to see Elliot stood in the doorway.

'Is it your lunch break soon?' He asked, holding up a picnic basket. She wanted to stay annoyed at him for interrupting her but how could she when he was stood there looking so handsome and with lunch in hand?

'Let me just finish valuing this item, take a seat.' Prue pointed Elliot towards an antique church pew that was pushed up against the back wall. As he took his seat she turned her attention back to the tea set that she was mid-valuation. Prue was trying to focus on the markings, however her mind kept wandering as to who had drunk from these cups and what conversations they had been party to. They were steeped in history and Prue couldn't reign her imagination in.

'Come on Prue, focus!' Elliot called from his seat, he could see the look that had crossed her face and he knew she was no longer concentrating on her work.

'Sorry!' Prue called back and forced herself to focus on the task at hand. She could daydream about who had drunk from these cups later.

It was a Saturday morning and the auction house had just been instructed to value and sell the contents of an entire house and so Prue was having to work this weekend. She didn't mind though, she was loving every second of her new job. After their trip to Brighton, Prue had been given the details of a local auction house that had recently been closed down and so after some research Prue had bought the place and re-employed all of the staff. Everyone had been grateful to have their job back and under Prue's enthusiastic management the place was now thriving. Prue could barely keep up with the valuations and the auctions were always full with people either looking for a bargain or just intrigued to see what the Clemonte's new business venture looked like. Either way, nobody ever left empty handed.

'Finished!' Prue finally announced as she closed the catalogue she was working on and turned around to give Elliot a huge smile. She was very happy to see him, he had still been asleep when she left that morning.

'Come on, let's go and eat.'

The auction house was set in a Tudor cottage with beautiful gardens and so they took their picnic outside. It was an unusually warm October day and would probably be their last chance to have a picnic outside until the following Spring.

'How's your mum?' Prue asked before she took a bite of her cheese and chutney doorstop. Elliot had bought the picnic from the cafe, rather than make it himself.

'She's fine. Everything is finally unpacked and your father is helping her build some of the furniture she ordered.' Elliot wiggled his eyebrows at Prue and she giggled before throwing her napkin at him. Robert and Maggie had been spending an increasing amount of time together, both of them enjoying some company as they healed their hearts.

'Does this mean you'll be moving back to your cottage?' Prue didn't want to ask the question but she knew she had to, the thought of Elliot leaving and going back to an empty manor each night made her want to cry. The renovations at Maggie's cottage had taken longer than expected due to some structural work that needed to be completed. Because of that Maggie had been staying at Elliot's cottage, whilst Elliot had moved into the manor with Prue.

'I don't have to move back, unless you want me to?' Elliot's usually self-assured manor was suddenly overshadowed by a look of doubt that crossed his face.

'I'd like you to stay at the manor.' Prue smiled as she watched the doubt leave his face and he leant over to kiss her.

Her life was unrecognisable from when she first arrived in the village. Here she was running her own auction house and with Elliot to go home to every night. *The Vintage Bookshop of Memories* was thriving under Maggie's watchful eye and her father often worked there at the weekend too. Whenever Prue wanted a break from life she popped into the bookshop and curled up with a book. These days she also had her father around, she had even called him dad the other evening. She hadn't meant to, it had just naturally slipped out but they had both smiled and not made a big deal of it. Carol was also ecstatic to have her nephew back in the village and to be able to acknowledge Prue as family. The future was unknown but Prue knew that from now on whatever happened she would have Elliot by her side and her father would always be there to support her. She was happy and she only hoped that her mother and grandmother would be proud of her. If it wasn't for that little bookshop she most likely wouldn't have unearthed all those secrets and memories and her life wouldn't be the way it was today.

The End.

BOOKS BY THIS AUTHOR

The Balance Between Life And Death

The balance between life and death can be precarious. Ana Adams wakes up every morning, goes to work and comes home at night to her dog. That doesn't mean she's living. After suffering the worst pain imaginable Ana is trying to make it through each day. The smile on her face means nothing, all that matters is the turmoil that is going on inside her head.

As Ana learns to open up to others and embarks on a new relationship she finds that letting life in is harder than she anticipated. Perhaps she's moved too fast and needs to focus on healing before opening herself up to more pain and disappointment.

Will Ana learn her lesson or will it be too late for her?

This novella focuses on the importance of putting your mental health first.
A reminder that you never know what someone is hiding beneath their smile.

CHRISTMAS AT THE VINTAGE BOOKSHOP OF MEMORIES

Coming November 2020.

Printed in Poland
by Amazon Fulfillment
Poland Sp. z o.o., Wrocław